新月集

The
Crescent
Moon

泰戈爾 著
Rabindranath Tagore

余淑慧、余淑娟、陳茂嘉 譯

推薦序

文／徐國能（作家）

　　有一些詩，無論甚麼時候讀，都有新的理解和感悟，這才發現自己又老了一些，又世故了一些。手捧《新月集》這本小書，字跡新鑄，意象如昨，那些輕濤或白花，依舊拍打四季，香成夢裡的四月天。我一面閱讀，卻不免想起這些詩句經歷童年的亂讀、少年的誤讀和青年的有所為而讀，中年重溫，隨之而來的，竟是對於過去的一點懷念，匆匆歲月，在一盞茶的時光裡片刻忘我，詩讓思念悠長，卻使感慨輕易。

　　過去我讀的是糜文開、糜榴麗的譯本，現在網路多是鄭振鐸的翻譯；如今又有了新的譯本，代表這本小書仍然在新時代裡感動一代人的心靈，裡面的情懷與哲理，像恆河的流水一樣，幽靜而清涼地流過乾渴的大地。

　　《新月集》寫的是孩子，有些作品模擬孩子的語氣說話，有些則是一個父親對孩子傾訴的神氣；或是純粹歌詠，那天真的懷抱是如何地將這汙濁世界重新洗滌，見證人間尚有值得的理由。或說詩中的孩子其實象徵純樸自然，那無邪的動作與看似幼稚的思想，其實正相對於人類過度文明的制約社會，已經無法理解大自然的真理。詩集第一篇〈家園〉說：「**這無數的家園裡有搖籃床鋪，有母親的心思，有黃昏的燈火和幼小的生命——洋溢著歡樂，卻不知歡樂對這世界有何價值的幼小生**

命。」且讓我自問，我能在一朵清晨的牽牛花中看見甚麼？我能在林間眾鳥雜噪的聊中聽見甚麼？能否珍惜每一次相遇，或是理解那些無言告別深藏的義理？《新月集》非常輕，像一隻水黽滑過湖沼，留下極淡的漣漪，但在我的心中，似也留下非常輕、且難以言喻的感動。

《新月集》的美不同於《漂鳥集》。《漂鳥集》是哲思悠遠的格言，揭示大自然無意流露的偉大智慧；《新月集》則屬於豐富溫柔的散文詩，在描述孩子與大人的互動中，點染那些要非常細心才能體會的幽情；例如〈香巴花〉一篇，〈仙境〉一篇，在眞與幻之間，揭示了苦於現實的人間需要一點童心。

新譯《新月集》有很多優點，準確無瑕，輕淺明朗，非常符合全書本身的主題思想，稍有爭議的部分也用註腳的方式，使全書既保持了詩的語言，又兼顧涵義，深入肌理。兩位余小姐的譯文如：「**在大千世界無止無盡的海灘上，孩童相聚。暴風雨在無路的天空胡亂行走，船隻在無軌的水上沉沒。死亡遍在，孩童嬉戲。在大千世界無止無盡的海灘上，孩童的聚會令人讚嘆。**」簡約的文字，將孩子瀕臨巨大死亡卻能安然自怡的生命情調譯得非常傳神。

《新月集》展現了泰戈爾獨特的詩心和才華，是文學國度裡可望而不可摘的天邊新月，晶瑩、冰涼而悠遠。反覆讀著這些詩句，驚覺人間輪迴的緣分，是何其廣大奧妙，而詩，卻包容了這一切。

〔譯序〕

一彎新月的光輝：
泰戈爾《新月集》的影響與翻譯

文／余淑慧、余淑娟

　　《新月集》（*The Crescent Moon*）是諾貝爾文學獎得主泰戈爾（Rabindranath Tagore, 1861-1941）的第二部英文詩集。這部詩集收錄四十首詩，其中有作者譯自孟加拉語《兒童集》（*Shishu*, 1903）的舊作，也有作者另以英文撰述的新作。這四十首以幼兒和孩童為主題的作品，全部整編在「新月」名下，作者的立意和用心格外引人深思。

新月的意義

　　「新月」是一種月相變化。在月圓月缺的過程中，一彎弦月總是予人許多想像。在印度，新月是重要的文化象徵，例如萬民慶祝的排燈節或屠妖節（Deepavali）就選在新月的夜晚舉行，以寄寓「光明驅走黑暗，善良戰勝邪惡」的意蘊。印度的重視新月，追根究柢和濕婆（Shiva）信仰相關。濕婆是印度教三大神祇之一，主司毀滅。但是由於毀滅與再生是一體的兩面，濕婆因此兼具毀滅、創造和轉化的神力。具體而論，祂頭飾上的一

彎新月，便是這一創造與轉化的象徵。

　　《新月集》兩度提到新月，即第三首的〈起源〉和第四首的〈寶寶之道〉。〈起源〉描寫「新月皎潔年輕的光」，落在「秋雲逐漸消逝的邊緣」時，寶寶的笑容就在這一刻誕生；新月與秋雲在此形成對比，雲的散逸烘托新月之代表新生。〈寶寶之道〉則提到寶寶入世前，本來住在「小小的新月國度裡」，自由自在，無憂無慮，完全「沒有任何約束」。由此觀之，新月似乎與新生兒有所聯繫，暗示幼小生命的初始與新生。換言之，《新月集》以新月為名，箇中即蘊藏著轉化與新生的創造觀。

《新月集》的寫作主題

　　《新月集》以兒童為主題，文字淺顯平易，再加上「新月」這個語詞本身蘊含的文化想像，所以常被解讀成童詩，或專為兒童而寫的詩集。就作品本身的敘事角度來看，《新月集》有十九首是從兒童的角度出發；換言之，兒童確實是《新月集》最重要的主角[1]。大致上，這十九首作品以孩童的視角摹形狀物，刻劃孩童心理，表現兒童世界的繽紛生趣與豐富想像，例如〈天文學家〉、〈雲朵和波浪〉、〈仙境〉、〈紙船〉、〈壞郵差〉、

---

1. 這十九首以兒童觀點寫作的詩，依序是第 13、14、15、16、17、19、20、21、22、23、24、25、26、27、28、29、30、31 與 32 首。

〈十二點〉等即是。其中〈十二點〉即藉一個不想在中午繼續唸書的小孩，扣問身為大人的母親為何無法突破黑夜與白天的侷限，把中午十二點想像成午夜十二點（因為到了夜晚他就不用唸書了）。他試圖說服母親的方式是：既然十二點「可以在夜晚降臨」，那麼「為甚麼夜晚不能在十二點降臨」？短短數行，小孩無拘無束的想像力躍然紙上，而小孩看待時間的靈活態度也十分有趣。

　　至於其他二十一首作品，儘管視角不同，但觀看的對象依然是孩童的世界。這類詩又可細分兩類：一是以全知的角度來描寫兒童與世界的關係，例如〈家園〉、〈海灘上〉、〈最後的交易〉等。這類詩裡的孩童除了作為孩童之外，同時也可視為人類的象徵。例如〈海灘上〉描寫一群孩童在海邊歡聚，然而詩人除了書寫生的歡聚，也不忘點出死亡的訊息。若從象徵的角度看，塵世猶如大海，「死亡遍在」，眾生卻如稚兒，兀自歡樂聚集，兀自歌舞嬉戲。

　　另一類則是從父母個體的角度來描寫孩童的世界。這類詩作，有的明顯出自父親的觀點，如〈玩具〉、〈不為人知的盛典〉、〈禮物〉、〈召喚〉等；有的視角就不那麼清楚，可能是父親，也可能是母親，或兩者兼具。這類詩作大致表現父母對孩子的愛、大人對小孩世界的羨慕，或者呈現大人與小孩的觀點差異，例如〈玩具〉一詩即表現兒童僅透過想像力，即可把泥巴與斷木殘枝

變成好玩的遊戲，大人卻深陷在金錢世界裡，只知無聊地加減乘除，卻忘了功名財富的追逐，到頭來也只是遊戲一場。

詩人筆下的兒童世界並不總是歡樂美好。詩集收入一首很特別的詩，題爲〈召喚〉；事實上，這是一首悼亡詩，描寫一位父親苦苦呼喚離世的女兒歸來。詩分三段，首段言夜已深沉，次段言花開正盛，三段言母愛滿溢，以此三者力勸亡魂歸來。因爲夜已深沉花正開盛母愛滿溢，亡魂此時若只是悄悄回來，向母親討個親親或帶走一朵小花，根本不會有人看見，也不會有人在意或者「妒恨」。這首詩通篇無一字提到愛，無一字提到思念，然而全篇無一字不是愛，無一字不是思念，讀來十分令人動容。[2]

爲大人而寫的希望之歌

回到文前的問題。《新月集》既然主要以兒童爲書寫主題，那麼這部詩集是不是一部童詩？或爲兒童而寫的集子？早年譯介泰戈爾作品的鄭振鐸，曾把《新月集》

---

2. 《新月集》共收入三首悼亡詩，另外兩首是〈我的歌〉和〈結束〉。這幾首詩有可能是泰戈爾本身的經歷；在發表《新月集》之前，他經歷了一連串家人離世之痛。他的妻子在一九〇二年過世，第二年長女過世，一九〇五年他的父親往生，過了兩年，他的大兒子也英年早逝，追隨其祖父與母姊於地下。

比擬為「安徒生的童話」，認為詩中充滿「不可測的魔力」；只要一翻開詩集，即可獲得一對「有魔力的翅膀」，助人掙脫苦悶的現實，飛入兒童「美靜天真」的「新月之國」，忘卻成人世界的算計與猜疑。但在譯序末尾，序作者亦提到《新月集》雖然描寫兒童的生活與心理，但「決非為兒童而作」[3]。換言之，這部詩集雖然寫的是兒童，但卻不是專為兒童而寫，當然也不是童詩。這話是對的。但是要進一步了解這部詩集，我們或許可以先探討對泰戈爾而言，「兒童」究竟代表甚麼意義。

如果先從知人論「詩」的角度來看，「兒童」這個主題對泰戈爾具有兩層特殊的意義。第一，兒童代表自然，抑或兒童就是自然，而自然即意謂著自由。對泰戈爾而言，描寫兒童，亦即描寫自然，亦即描寫自由的心靈。在〈我的學校〉（"My School"）一文中，他曾表示他「心裡住著一個孩童」，以此況喻其靈魂的自由。因此，「孩童」在這部詩集裡可謂扮演了雙重的角色，一個是具體的、現實人生裡的孩童——可能是詩人的小孩，也可能是他人的小孩；另一個角色則是孩童所代表的意義，包括自然與自由的靈魂。

如果參照詩人的其他作品，我們亦可知對詩人來說，「孩童」還代表了人類的未來和希望。在《漂鳥集》第77首詩裡，我們可以很清楚地看到這一點：

每個孩子的誕生都捎來一則訊息：神對人類尚
未感到絕望。

Every child comes with the message that God is
not yet discouraged of man.

　　換句話說，每一個孩子的出生都宣告著人類的希望
和未來。綜合前述幾點，《新月集》描寫的固然是孩童
的世界，然而詩人藉之歌詠的也是新生、自由與希望。
誠如與泰戈爾情誼深厚的現代詩人徐志摩所說的，那「纖
弱的一彎」新月（或孩童），其實「懷抱著未來的圓滿」，
其中暗喻著許多未來的可能[4]。如此說來，若把《新月集》
視為泰戈爾為大人而寫的希望之歌，這或許一點也不為
過吧。[5]

---

3. 鄭振鐸，〈譯者自序〉，收在《泰戈爾詩選》（湖南人民出版社，1981
年），頁 61。

4. 徐志摩，〈新月的態度〉，《新月月刊》創刊號頁 3-10，1928 年；或參
見《徐志摩全集補編 3 ── 散文集》（香港：商務印書館，1993 年），
頁 357。

5. 作家蘇雪林曾為糜文開等譯的《泰戈爾詩集》寫了一篇序，在此序文
中，蘇雪林提到泰戈爾的《新月集》是一個「閃著琥珀色奇光的兒童
王國」，裡頭設了一場盛宴，任何人只須「帶著一顆赤裸的『童心』」，
即可參加。由此可知蘇雪林、糜文開也不認為這是一部童詩。見蘇雪林，
〈序〉，收在《泰戈爾詩集》（台北：三民書局股份有限公司，2013 年），
頁 92。

新月映照下的中文世界

　　就用字而論，泰戈爾的英文詩固然少有生澀難字，讀來也平易近人，不過在中文世界裡，他的詩最初並不是以現代白話文來完整呈現，而是一、二首零星地出現在報刊雜誌，例如一九一五年，陳獨秀翻譯、刊在《青年雜誌》的四首《吉檀迦利》（Gitanjali），其所選用的文體即是五言古詩。到了一九一八年，詩人劉半農才以白話文翻譯了泰戈爾的七首詩，其中有兩首即來自《新月集》。

　　至於《新月集》全譯本的問世，則要等到一九二三年，鄭振鐸翻譯出版的版本[6]。根據鄭振鐸的譯序，他是在許地山的引介之下，初次接觸泰戈爾的作品，並對泰戈爾的詩產生濃厚的興趣，尤其是《新月集》。不久，許地山送給他一本《新月集》，並鼓勵他以「新妍流露」的文體來對譯。此後，許地山以「古奧」的文體翻譯《吉檀迦利》，鄭振鐸則以「新妍流露」的白話翻譯《新月集》，譯成即陸續發表在《小說月報》。可惜的是，兩人的這個計畫固然有最初的譯介之功，但是當時卻未能如期完成。許地山終究放棄了《吉》的譯介，幸好輾轉數年之後，鄭振鐸藉由補譯，終於把《新月集》譯全。[7]

中文現代詩的「新月」：從月刊到詩派

　　二十世紀初，現代詩的初期實踐深受域外詩學的影響，譬如冰心即說過泰戈爾是她「青年時代最愛慕的外國詩人」[8]。不過，最耐人尋味的是「新月」一詞在華語世界留下的影響：或許「新月」一詞竟是新月詩派得名之緣起。

　　一九二七年，徐志摩提議創建新月雜誌。第二年，徐志摩、聞一多、饒孟侃三人主編的《新月》月刊問世。據梁實秋回憶，「新月」之命名是徐志摩的意思，而當中的關鍵正是泰戈爾[9]。徐志摩與泰戈爾情誼深厚；泰戈爾生病時，徐志摩曾感嘆詩人老去，惋惜詩人遭受世人排斥的悲哀，並把詩人與孔子相提並論[10]。如此深切的感悟，足見徐志摩對泰戈爾的認同，以及泰戈爾在他心中的地位。

　　除了與泰戈爾有所聯繫之外，「新月」還另有一層

---

6. 石真，〈前言〉，《泰戈爾詩選》（湖南人民出版社，1981年），頁1。
7. 鄭振鐸，〈譯者自序〉，《泰戈爾詩選》（湖南人民出版社，1981年），頁60-61。
8. 冰心，〈《泰戈爾詩選》譯者序〉，收在張光璘編著，《中國名家論泰戈爾》（北京：中國華僑出版社，1994年），頁175。
9. 梁實秋，〈憶「新月」〉，徐志摩編，《新月選集·翻譯小說》（台北：喜美出版社，1980年），頁1-13。
10. 郁達夫，〈志摩在回憶裡〉，《新月選集·散文》（台北：喜美出版社，1980年），頁240-246。

意義。根據徐志摩在《新月》月刊創刊號上的說法：「新月」之得名，不是因為「新月社」，不是因為「新月書店」，而是因為「新月」雖然「纖弱」，卻「懷抱著未來的圓滿」[11]；換句話說，在現代文學多變的二十世紀初，《新月》月刊以未來為念，不僅刊載新詩，也刊載散文、小說、評論、思想與翻譯，顯示月刊的格局宏大，是一個結合了文藝、學術與理想的園地，希望為「時代的生命添厚一些光輝」。[12]

　　以上是《新月》月刊的創建始末。至於現代詩壇之出現新月詩派，《新月詩選》扮演的角色至關重要。一九三一年，陳夢家承徐志摩之託，精選十八家詩人的八十首作品，編成《新月詩選》。陳氏整合一九二〇～三〇年間的詩歌，指出這類詩歌具有雙重創造的涵意：一是表現手法上的創新；二是靈感方面新印象的獲取，並主張詩歌當追求本質的醇正、技巧的周密和格律的謹嚴。這當中的新印象和新手法之創造，似乎與「新月」的起始意義脫離不了關係。

《新月集》的寫作方式與翻譯策略

　　泰戈爾六部英文詩集中，最廣為人知的莫過於《漂鳥集》和《新月集》。二〇一八年，我們翻譯了《漂鳥集》，如今接續翻譯《新月集》。兩相比較之下，深感兩部作品的創作風格差異極大，迥然不同。

在形式上，《漂鳥集》都是短詩，從一行到三行不等。行數雖少，種種文學技巧如文字與意象的對稱、用韻、文字遊戲等卻用得極為頻繁，幾乎每一首每一行都施以文學技巧的魔術，使之形象鮮明、讀來朗朗上口。但是《新月集》不同；收入《新月集》的四十首詩，大部分都是十行以上的長詩，其中最短的一首也有六行。相對於《漂鳥集》在文學技巧方面的機關用盡，《新月集》這部抒情的散文詩顯得天然流暢，平易近人。除了行數長短不一，在語言和意象的使用上亦顯得十分節制，只有少許的對稱，少許的文字遊戲，少許的頭韻，而且幾乎不用尾韻。真要論及技巧，唯一比較明顯的是每隔幾行就會重複某個句子，有時是整句重複，有時是部份重複，頗像《詩經》裡的複沓手法。這樣的重複與部份重複，除了形成自然的段落或詩節（stanza）之外，也創造了意義的連續與語言的流動，形成某種詠嘆歌吟的閱讀效果。

確立《新月集》的寫作風格之後，我們擬定了兩個翻譯策略。第一是尊重泰戈爾對詩的看法──詩的「怎麼寫」有時候比「寫甚麼」更為重要，因此在形式上我們極力追摹，可以保留的形式盡量予以保留，例如維持

---

11. 參見注 4。
12. 同上註。

散文詩長長短短的形式，行文中若遇到詩人有意創造的重複或複沓亦極力保留。至於那些無法保留與追摹的部份，我們則沿用泰戈爾本人對翻譯的看法，亦即讓譯文在譯語世界裡藉譯語文字的固有特質「重生」（rebirth），在譯語世界另行創造新的生命。[13]

　　之所以如此制定這第二個策略，我們得回到泰戈爾本人的翻譯經歷與翻譯觀。據泰戈爾的回憶錄，我們知道他早年曾與兄姊、同輩親戚組織劇團，合辦報刊雜誌來發表他們創作或翻譯的劇本、小說、詩歌或評論。其中有一篇文章特別提到他每日下午四點放學回家，晚上七點就有家庭教師來給他上英文課，其中一項功課就是把《馬克白》（Macbeth）翻譯成孟加拉文。第一次訪英留學，他隨身帶著自己英譯的詩集，並且在海旅途中，日日修改潤飾。這部翻譯詩集本來只是一份送給英國友人的禮物，沒想到竟然引起英國友人的讚嘆，將之推薦給葉慈（William Butler Yeats），更沒想到葉慈大為感動，為之潤稿作序並推薦出版，因而種下了日後詩人獲得諾貝爾文學獎的因緣。這是一段人盡皆知的文壇與譯壇佳話。

　　然而鮮為人知的是：泰戈爾對翻譯始終深感興趣。除了創作，他同時也持續兼做翻譯，鍛鍊自己的詩藝。從他的書信與散文來看，他不但在英國期間時常為友人翻譯自己的詩作或印度文學作品，返回印度之後，他一

有空就到書店找書，把他認為簡單的英詩譯成孟加拉文，從中學習英詩的創作技巧。一九一八年，在一封寫給友人的信裡，我們看到他對譯詩的看法：

當初我沒把那些詩譯成韻體，那是因為我對英文的掌握還不夠精熟。不過，現在我越來越能接受自己的種種侷限，而且我也漸漸了解英語散文的神奇力量。結構勻稱的英語散文所具有的清晰，力量和音樂性這些特質使我的翻譯任務——把孟加拉詩譯成英語散文——充滿愉悅。譯詩的時候，我們應該坦然放棄重現原文詩歌在音韻方面的種種（情感）暗示，代之以（新的）表達工具所蘊含的新特質。英語散文似乎有一種魔法，使我的孟加拉詩歌轉化成另一種形式不同的原作。因此，我不僅感到滿意，而且非常樂於協助我的孟加拉詩歌，使之重生於英語散文之中，即使我並不十分確知這一任務到底有多成功。[14]

---

13. 「重生」是一九一八年，泰戈爾寫給安德森（James Drummond Anderson）的信裡所用的語詞。見 Alam F. & Chakravarty R.. (ed. 2011). *The Essential Tagore.* England: The Belknap Press of Harvard University Press， 頁 107。

這段話除了讓我們看到泰戈爾好學不懈的謙虛精神之外，最引人注目的是他對翻譯／語言所抱持的開放態度。經歷多年的翻譯經驗之後，詩人提出在譯詩的過程，我們「應該坦然放棄重現原文詩歌在音韻方面的種種（情感）暗示，代之以（新的）表達工具所蘊含的新特質」。落在英中譯詩的情境裡，例如中文本無頭韻，與其強求，不如尋找中文這一新的表達工具所擁有的特質（例如尾韻），並坦然以之代換頭韻。這是一個長期生活在雙語環境，擁有豐富譯歷經驗的人才有可能說出來的話。這種承認語言本身各自的差異與限制的態度，若就西方翻譯理論史的角度看，那已經是二十世紀七〇年代譯學（Translation Studies）發展起來之後的事了。所謂以新的特質代換原文音韻上的種種暗示，此說法與翻譯理論家勒弗維爾（André Lefevere）在一九九〇年代所提到的「補償說」也頗有幾分相似之處；至於讓原文在譯語世界裡「重生」這一說法，則讓人忍不住想到班雅明（Walter Benjamin）：一九二三年，班雅明譯完波特萊爾（Baudelaire）的作品之後，寫了一篇譯序談到譯文是原文的「來生」（afterlife）[15]。如果有一個神奇的空間讓這三個人共聚一堂，真不知會相互激發出哪些譯論方面的光亮！

　　除了詩歌文本的翻譯，我們也為這部《新月集》增添了注解，舉凡涉及印度文化或文學典故的專有名詞，

或具有特殊意義的植物，我們都儘可能地附上注解。另外無法納入文本的譯／異文，也以腳注嘗試解釋其緣由。

14. 這段書信是我翻譯的，信裡提到的「那些詩」是指《吉檀迦利》；其出處同前注，頁 107。這封信的原文如下： It was the want of mastery in your language that originally prevented me from trying English meters in my translations. But now I have grown reconciled to my limitations through which I have come to know the wonderful power of English prose. The clearness, strength and the suggestive music of well-balanced English sentences make it a delightful task for me to mould my Bengali poems into English prose form. I think one should frankly give up the attempt at reproducing in a translation the lyrical suggestions of the original verse and substitute in their place some new quality inherent in the new vehicle of expression. In English prose there is a magic which seems to transmute my Bengali verses into something which is original again in a different manner. Therefore it not only satisfies but gives me delight to assist my poems in their English rebirth though I am far from being confident in the success of my task.

15. 班雅明所譯的作品是波特萊爾的《巴黎群像》（*Tableaux Parisiens*），其所寫的譯序題為〈譯者的天職〉（"The Task of the Translator"）。這篇文章見 Zohn, H (tr. 1968). "The Task of the Translator," in Walter Benjamin, *Illuminations*. New York: Harcourt, Brace and World.

1

家園 [1]

◆

THE HOME

　我獨自在橫越田間的小路漫步，夕陽正藏起最後的金光，像個守財奴。

　白晝墜入黑暗，越來越見深沉；收割後的田空蕩蕩一片，大地悄無聲息。

　突然間，有個男孩唱起歌來，音聲高亢，直飄天際。他在黑暗中行走，不爲人見，只留下歌的餘音，裊裊穿透黃昏的靜謐。

　他的家座落在那片鄉間荒地的盡頭，蔗田的另一邊，藏在芭蕉樹與瘦高的檳榔樹，還有椰子樹與麵包樹深深的樹影裡。

我在途中停下腳步，獨自在星光下佇立片刻。暮色漸濃的大地在我眼前伸展，漸漸環抱家園無數。這無數的家園裡有搖籃床鋪，有母親的心思，有黃昏的燈火和幼小的生命——洋溢著歡樂，卻不知歡樂對這世界有何價值的幼小生命。[2]

---

1. 這部詩集的前面三首詩〈家園〉、〈海灘上〉與〈源頭〉又見於作者另一部英文詩集《吉檀迦利》（*Gitanji*），分別是後者的第 60、61 和第 62 首。詩的內容與辭句一模一樣，唯一的差異是收入《吉檀迦利》的三首詩沒有標題。

2. 〈家園〉詩分五段，描寫一位散步者在黃昏轉入黑夜的時刻，獨自走入空蕩蕩、悄然無聲的田野。第三段是個轉折，因為此時突然有一男孩的歌聲嘹亮地直飄天際，引得散步者不由得回首望向歌者，但是詩人說歌者行走在黑暗裡，渺不可得；可以看見的，只有藏在重重樹影下的無數家園與人間燈火。這第三段是個分界點，自然風景與人間燈火在此形成對比；無聲的自然與高歌的男孩也是一個對照，介於這兩種對照中的敘述者「我」，其身分十分神祕，耐人尋味。至於詩法，泰戈爾用了他擅長的文字遊戲（glad with a gladness）和頭韻，尤其頭韻最明顯，例如第二行：The daylight sank deeper and deeper into the darkness, and the widowed land, whose harvest had been reaped, lay silent，句中的 daylight，deeper，darkness 顯然押了頭韻 /d/；第三行前半句 Suddenly a boy's shrill voice rose into the sky，句中的 suddenly，shrill 和 sky 則押了頭韻 /s/。中文無法追摹此種字法與用韻法，只能嘗試以疊詞和句中韻對譯，希望多少營造一點音韻效果。

I PACED alone on the road across the field while the sunset was hiding its last gold like a miser.

The daylight sank deeper and deeper into the darkness, and the widowed land, whose harvest had been reaped, lay silent.

Suddenly a boy's shrill voice rose into the sky. He traversed the dark unseen, leaving the track of his song across the hush of the evening.

His village home lay there at the end of the waste land, beyond the sugar-cane field, hidden among the shadows of the banana and the slender areca palm, the cocoa-nut and the dark green jack-fruit trees.

I stopped for a moment in my lonely way under the starlight, and saw spread before me the darkened earth surrounding with her arms countless homes furnished with cradles and beds, mothers' hearts and evening lamps, and young lives glad with a gladness that knows nothing of its value for the world.

2

海灘上

◆

ON THE SEASHORE

在大千世界無止無盡的海灘上，孩童相聚。[3]

廣袤的天在他們頭上靜止不動，不息的水在他們腳邊喧鬧不停。在大千世界無止無盡的海灘上，孩童相聚，相互招呼，一起跳舞。

他們用沙子蓋屋，用空貝殼玩遊戲。他們把枯葉編成小船，笑著讓小船漂向遼闊的大海。在大千世界無止無盡的海灘上，孩童嬉戲。

他們不知如何游泳，他們不知如何撒網。採珠人入海採珠，商人遠航經商。孩童收集許多小圓石，隨即將之丟棄；他們不尋求隱匿的寶藏——他們不知如何撒網。

大海笑著掀起澎湃的浪，岸上灰白色的點點閃光是海灘的微笑。致命的波濤對孩童唱著沒有意義的歌，幾乎就像推著搖籃的母親。大海陪著孩童嬉戲，岸上灰白色的點點閃光是海灘的微笑。

在大千世界無止無盡的海灘上，孩童相聚。暴風雨在無路的天空胡亂行走，船隻在無軌的水上沉沒。死亡遍在，孩童嬉戲。在大千世界無止無盡的海灘上，孩童的相聚令人讚嘆。

---

3. 這首詩本無標題，這裡的標題取自第一行前三個字。事實上，第一行 "On the seashore of endless worlds children meet" 也是全詩最重要的一行，因為這一行以少許的變化在詩中重複了五次，末段甚至有一句與這一行重複，完全沒有任何變化。這樣的重複當然是刻意的，目的在於營造一種迴環往復，感慨萬千的效果。中文翻譯盡量保留這一特色，以「在大千世界無止無盡的海灘上，孩童相聚」追仿。另一種重複藏在字尾的運用上。詩歌在第一句的 endless 之後，相續提出五個以 "less" 為結尾的語詞如 motionless、restless、meaningless、pathless、trackless 來貫串全詩。這當然也是詩人的刻意之筆，或詩人的創作方式之一。但是礙於中文沒有相應的構詞方式，我們嘗試以「無止無盡」、「不動」、「不停」來追仿一二。

O N the seashore of endless worlds children meet.

The infinite sky is motionless overhead and the restless water is boisterous. On the seashore of endless worlds the children meet with shouts and dances.

They build their houses with sand, and they play with empty shells. With withered leaves they weave their boats and smilingly float them on the vast deep. Children have their play on the seashore of worlds.

They know not how to swim, they know not how to cast nets.Pearl-fishers dive for pearls, merchants sail in their ships, while children gather pebbles and scatter them again. They seek not for hidden treasures, they know not how to cast nets.

The sea surges up with laughter, and pale gleams the smile of the sea-beach. Death-dealing waves sing meaningless ballads to the children, even like a mother while rocking her baby's cradle. The sea plays with children, and pale gleams the smile of the sea-beach.

On the seashore of endless worlds children meet. Tempest roams in the pathless sky, ships are wrecked in the trackless water, death is abroad and children play. On the seashore of endless worlds is the great meeting of children.

3

源頭 [4]

◆

THE SOURCE

睡神掠過寶寶的雙眼──有人知道睡神從哪兒來？有
的，相傳睡神就住在仙子村。村子籠罩在森林重重的樹
影裡，只有螢火蟲黯淡的光照亮；那裡懸著兩朵羞怯迷
人的蓓蕾。睡神就打從那兒來，來親寶寶的雙眼。

寶寶入眠時，笑容掠過雙唇──有人知道這笑容從哪
兒來？有的，相傳新月皎潔年輕的光一照上秋雲逐漸消
逝的邊緣，笑容就在那裡首次誕生，誕生在朝露滌淨的
晨夢裡──寶寶入眠時，那一抹掠過他唇邊的笑容。

可愛輕柔的朝氣如花綻放在寶寶的手腳上──有人
知道這朝氣向來藏在哪兒？有的，當母親還是少女時，
這朝氣就藏在她心裡，藏在愛情那溫柔而沉默的奧祕裡

——那股輕柔可愛，綻放在寶寶手腳上的朝氣。

---

4. 這首詩本無標題，作者在這裡可能是根據詩的內容，為之安上〈源頭〉這一標題；詩分三段，以設問法為架構，追問並回答具體的「睡眠」、「笑容」，到抽象的「朝氣」或生命力的源頭，意境優美，充滿童話般的想像力。詩集的「新月」（crescent moon）一詞，首度出現在這一首詩裡；至於「新月」的可能意涵，請參閱〈譯序〉。

THE sleep that flits on baby's eyes--does anybody know from where it comes? Yes, there is a rumour that it has its dwelling where, in the fairy village among shadows of the forest dimly lit with glow-worms, there hang two shy buds of enchantment. From there it comes to kiss baby's eyes.

The smile that flickers on baby's lips when he sleeps — does anybody know where it was born? Yes, there is a rumour that a young pale beam of a crescent moon touched the edge of a vanishing autumn cloud, and there the smile was first born in the dream of a dew-washed morning--the smile that flickers on baby's lips when he sleeps.

The sweet, soft freshness that blooms on baby's limbs — does anybody know where it was hidden so long? Yes, when the mother was a young girl it lay pervading her heart in tender and silent mystery of love--the sweet, soft freshness that has bloomed on baby's limbs.

4

寶寶之道

◆

BABY'S WAY

只要寶寶願意，此時此刻就可飛上青天。

他不離開我們，並非沒有道理。[5]

他愛把頭枕在媽媽的胸口；看不到媽媽的蹤影，他一刻都無法忍受。

寶寶懂得所有智慧的語言，即便世上無人了解那些語言的意義。

他從來就不想說話，並非沒有道理。

他唯一想做的就是學會母親嘴裡說出的語言——這就是他看來如此純真的原因。

寶寶曾經擁有成堆的黃金和珍珠，但他卻像個乞丐般地來到這世間。

他喬裝成這副模樣入世，並非沒有道理。

這裸身的可愛小乞兒假裝全然無助，以此博取媽媽豐沛的愛。

在小小的新月國度裡，寶寶沒有任何約束。

如今他放棄了自由，並非沒有道理。

他知道媽媽心中有個小小的角落藏著無窮的喜悅；他知道依偎在媽媽懷裡，貼著媽媽親愛的臂膀遠比自由更為甜蜜。

寶寶過去住在幸福圓滿的樂土，他從來不知道哭泣。

如今他選擇了流淚，並非沒有道理。

雖然憑他可愛臉龐上的笑容，就能牽動媽媽的心，但他為微不足道的瑣事哭鬧，也織就了讓媽媽既憐又愛的兩重心情。

---

5. 「並非沒有道理」（It is not for nothing...）這個句型在這首詩裡重複了五次，層層遞進地解釋寶寶來到人間、不想說話、化身為乞兒、放棄天界的自由，並選擇入世來流淚的理由。這是一種複沓，或每一次用字都有所變化的重複。中文翻譯盡量保持這一特色，但是因為中英句法的差異，中文將之調到句末，例如"It is not for nothing that he does not leave us"一句，我們的翻譯是：「他不離開我們，並非沒有道理。」

I F baby only wanted to, he could fly up to heaven this moment.

It is not for nothing that he does not leave us.

He loves to rest his head on mother's bosom, and cannot ever bear to lose sight of her.

Baby knows all manner of wise words, though few on earth can understand their meaning.

It is not for nothing that he never wants to speak.

The one thing he wants is to learn mother's words from mother's lips. That is why he looks so innocent.

Baby had a heap of gold and pearls, yet he came like a beggar on to this earth.

It is not for nothing he came in such a disguise.

This dear little naked mendicant pretends to be utterly helpless, so that he may beg for mother's wealth of love.

Baby was so free from every tie in the land of the tiny crescent moon.

It was not for nothing he gave up his freedom.

He knows that there is room for endless joy in mother's little corner of a heart, and it is sweeter far than liberty to be caught and pressed in her dear arms.

Baby never knew how to cry. He dwelt in the land of perfect bliss.

It is not for nothing he has chosen to shed tears.

Though with the smile of his dear face he draws mother's yearning heart to him, yet his little cries over tiny troubles weave the double bond of pity and love.

5

不為人知的表演盛會

◆

THE UNHEEDED PAGEANT

啊！孩子，是誰給你那小小的長袍染上顏色？是誰給你那可愛的手腳套上小小的紅色緊身衣？[6]

你一早就到院子裡玩，你一跑起來不是搖晃就是摔倒。

但是我的孩子，是誰給你那小小的長袍染上顏色？

我小小的生命花蕾，什麼事讓你笑得這麼開心？

媽媽一直站在門檻上，微笑著看你嬉戲。

她一拍手，手鐲就叮噹作響；你拿著竹竿跳舞，像個可愛的小小牧童。

我小小的生命花蕾，什麼事讓你笑得這麼開心？

噢，你這乞兒，你雙手抱著媽媽的脖子在求些什麼？

噢，貪婪的心，我是不是該摘下世界，放入你紅潤的小掌心，就像從天空摘下一顆果子？

噢，你這乞兒，你在求些什麼？

你腳鍊鈴鐺的叮鈴叮鈴聲，風快樂地帶走。

太陽露出微笑，照看著你梳洗。天空護著你，讓你在媽媽的臂彎裡沉睡；清晨躡手躡腳地來到你床邊，親吻你的眼。

你腳鍊的叮鈴叮鈴聲，風快樂地帶走。

夢境的仙子穿過了薄暮的天空，朝你飛來。
在你媽媽的心裡，世界之母在你身邊留有一席座位。
那個向星子奏樂的人，此刻拿著長笛站在你窗邊。
夢境的仙子穿過了薄暮的天空，朝你飛來。

6.　這首〈不為人知的表演盛會〉描寫小孩一早在院子裡的紅色泥地上學走路，因為還走不穩，不時跌倒，因此衣服和手腳都沾上了塵土的情景。詩中所謂的「緊身衣」（tunic），實指附著在小孩皮膚上的紅色塵土；當然也沒人給小孩穿的防髒連身長袍（frock）「染上顏色」──衣服染上泥土的顏色，其實只是因為小孩不斷跌倒的緣故。小孩學走路，弄得一身髒，這在尋常人眼裡，大概不是一件甚麼值得大書特書的事，但是詩人將之寫成一場「表演」，而且是「色彩繽紛、華麗炫耀的露天盛會」（pageant），其中有母親的鼓掌，還有風、陽光、天空來助陣，身為父親的詩人甚至想要摘下世界，猶如摘下一顆果子作為孩子的獎賞。孩子的一舉一動，果真是父母眼中的表演盛事。由於這種日常的「表演」，通常只有心中有愛的父母看得見，對於其他人，通常都是視而不見的小事，此所以這場表演盛事「不為人知」（unheeded）的緣故。

AH, who was it coloured that little frock, my child, and covered your sweet limbs with that little red tunic?

You have come out in the morning to play in the courtyard, tottering and tumbling as you run.

But who was it coloured that little frock, my child?

What is it makes you laugh, my little life-bud?

Mother smiles at you standing on the threshold.

She claps her hands and her bracelets jingle, and you dance with your bamboo stick in your hand like a tiny little shepherd.

But what is it makes you laugh, my little life-bud?

O beggar, what do you beg for, clinging to your mother's neck with both your hands?

O greedy heart, shall I pluck the world like a fruit from the sky to place it on your little rosy palm?

O beggar, what are you begging for?

The wind carries away in glee the tinkling of your anklet bells.

The sun smiles and watches your toilet. The sky watches over you when you sleep in your mother's arms, and the morning comes tiptoe to your bed and kisses your eyes.

The wind carries away in glee the tinkling of your anklet bells.

The fairy mistress of dreams is coming towards you, flying through the twilight sky.

The world-mother keeps her seat by you in your mother's heart.

He who plays his music to the stars is standing at your window with his flute.

And the fairy mistress of dreams is coming towards you, flying through the twilight sky.

6

睡眠竊賊

◆

SLEEP-STEALER

是誰偷走寶寶眼裡的睡眠？我一定要知道。

媽媽把水罐扣在腰際，走到鄰村汲水。

日正當午，孩子的遊戲時間已結束，池塘裡的鴨子已靜默。

牧童躺在榕樹蔭下，睡得正香甜。

白鷺沉靜肅穆地站在芒果林附近的沼澤裡。

睡眠竊賊就在這時飛來，迅速搶走了寶寶眼裡的睡眠。

媽媽回家，看到寶寶在房間的地上爬來爬去。

是誰偷走寶寶眼裡的睡眠？我一定要知道。我一定要找到她，把她用鍊子拴起。

我一定要去黑暗的山洞看看，那裡有一條小溪流過巨石和錯雜堆疊的小石。

　　我一定要去巴古拉樹叢那令人昏睡的樹蔭下找找；那裡有鴿子躲在一角咕咕叫，那裡有仙子的腳鍊在靜謐的星夜裡叮噹作響。

　　黃昏時分，我將偷偷探訪竹林細語喃喃的寧靜，那裡有螢火蟲在林中揮霍著光亮；我將詢問所有我遇到的生物：「睡眠竊賊住在哪裡？」

　　是誰偷走寶寶眼裡的睡眠？我一定要知道。

　　假如抓得到她，我難道不該好好給她一頓教訓？

　　我要突襲她的巢穴，看她把偷來的睡眠囤積在哪裡。

　　我要把睡眠全部搶回來，全部帶回家裡。

　　我要把她的雙翼牢牢縶起，把她放在河岸上，給她一根蘆桿，讓她在燈心草和睡蓮之間垂釣取樂。

　　黃昏市集結束的時候，村裡的小孩都在媽媽的膝上睡著了；這時夜鳥會在她的耳邊不住地嘲諷：「現在妳還能去偷誰的睡眠？」

WHO stole sleep from baby's eyes? I must know.

Clasping her pitcher to her waist mother went to fetch water from the village near by.

It was noon. The children's playtime was over; the ducks in the pond were silent.

The shepherd boy lay asleep under the shadow of the banyan tree.

The crane stood grave and still in the swamp near the mango grove.

In the meanwhile the Sleep-stealer came and, snatching sleep from baby's eyes, flew away.

When mother came back she found baby travelling the room over on all fours.

Who stole sleep from our baby's eyes? I must know. I must find her and chain her up.

I must look into that dark cave, where, through boulders and scowling stones, trickles a tiny stream.

I must search in the drowsy shade of the bakula grove, where pigeons coo in their corner, and fairies' anklets tinkle in the stillness of starry nights.

In the evening I will peep into the whispering silence of the bamboo forest, where fireflies squander their light, and will ask every creature I meet, "Can anybody tell me where the Sleep-stealer lives?"

Who stole sleep from baby's eyes? I must know.

Shouldn't I give her a good lesson if I could only catch her!

I would raid her nest and see where she hoards all her stolen sleep.

I would plunder it all, and carry it home.

I would bind her two wings securely, set her on the bank of the river, and then let her play at fishing with a reed among the rushes and water-lilies.

When the marketing is over in the evening, and the village children sit in their mothers' laps, then the night birds will mockingly din her ears with:

"Whose sleep will you steal now?"

7

開端

◆

THE BEGINNING

「我從哪兒來?妳在哪兒撿到我?」孩子問媽媽。

媽媽把孩子緊擁入懷,亦哭亦笑地答:「親愛的,你曾經藏在我心底,是我心底最大的想望。

你藏在我童年時代的玩偶裡;每天早上我用黏土捏塑神的形象,那時我就捏塑了你又同時捏碎了你。[7]

你和家裡的守護神一起供在神龕裡,每當我膜拜家裡的守護神,我也同時膜拜了你。

你一直藏在我所有的希望和愛裡——你藏在我的生命裡,也藏在我母親的生命裡。

守護我們家的不朽神靈把你抱在懷裡,撫育了你好幾個世紀。

在少女時代,我的心宛如花瓣綻放,你是繚繞在我心上的一縷芳香。

你的溫柔在我青春的四肢綻放,宛如日出前天上的一

道清輝。

　你是天堂的第一個寵兒，與晨光同時降生；你沿著世界的生命溪流漂游而下，最後停駐在我心頭。

　當我凝視你的臉，神奇的奧祕撼動著我：本屬一切的你，如今竟成為我的孩子。

　因為害怕失去你，我把你緊緊摟在胸前。

　到底是什麼樣的魔法，竟把這世間的珍寶送入我纖細的臂彎？」

---

7. 英文可以用前綴（prefix）與後綴（suffix）等來改變語詞的意義。泰戈爾很擅長於利用這一點，讓兩個有關連的語詞，同時在意義與音聲方面創造相應與逆反的效果。詩中第三行的 I made and unmade you then，其中 made 和 unmade 就是一例。中文難以再現這樣的語言特色，因而針對使用黏土的情境，加入「捏」字，使「那時我就捏塑了你又同時捏碎了你」譯文中的「塑」與「碎」產生對應。同樣的技法亦散見於《吉檀迦利》，例如第十三首的首二句：The song that I came to sing remains unsung to this day./ I have spent my days in stringing and unstringing my intrument；句中的 sing 與 unsung 對應，stringing 和 unstringing 對應。

"WHERE have I come from, where did you pick me up?" the baby asked its mother.

She answered half crying, half laughing, and clasping the baby to her breast, -- "You were hidden in my heart as its desire, my darling.

You were in the dolls of my childhood's games; and when with clay I made the image of my god every morning, I made and unmade you then.

You were enshrined with our household deity, in his worship I worshipped you.

In all my hopes and my loves, in my life, in the life of my mother you have lived.

In the lap of the deathless Spirit who rules our home you have been nursed for ages.

When in girlhood my heart was opening its petals, you hovered as a fragrance about it.

Your tender softness bloomed in my youthful limbs, like a glow in the sky before the sunrise.

Heaven's first darling, twin-born with the morning light, you have floated down the stream of the world's life, and at last you have stranded on my heart.

As I gaze on your face, mystery overwhelms me; you who belong to all have become mine.

For fear of losing you I hold you tight to my breast. What magic has snared the world's treasure in these slender arms of mine?"

8

孩子的世界

◆

BABY'S WORLD

在孩子心裡那個非常私密的世界裡，但願我能擁有一個寧靜的角落。

在那個世界裡，我知道星子會跟他說話，天空會俯身在他面前，用傻傻的雲和彩虹逗他開心。

那些看似不會說話，看似永遠不動的事物會悄悄爬到他窗前，為他帶來許多故事和色彩繽紛的玩具。

但願我能在橫越孩子心中的那條路上旅行，跨越所有的界限；

在那裡，信使替沒有歷史的諸王奔走，往來於王國與王國之間；

在那裡，**理性**把她的法則製成風箏，任其飛翔；在那裡，**眞理**鬆開束縛著事實的所有桎梏。[8]

8. 詩中的「理性」和「真理」以擬人化的手法展現，並以大寫（Reason/Truth）表示。中譯以粗體表示。

I WISH I could take a quiet corner in the heart of my baby's very own world.

I know it has stars that talk to him, and a sky that stoops down to his face to amuse him with its silly clouds and rainbows.

Those who make believe to be dumb, and look as if they never could move, come creeping to his window with their stories and with trays crowded with bright toys.

I wish I could travel by the road that crosses baby's mind, and out beyond all bounds;

Where messengers run errands for no cause between the kingdoms of kings of no history;

Where Reason makes kites of her laws and flies them, and Truth sets Fact free from its fetters.

9

時機與原因

◆

WHEN AND WHY

　　我的孩子，當我為你帶來色彩繽紛的玩具時，我終於明白雲朵和水面為甚麼會有那樣的色彩變化；我終於明白為什麼花朵要畫成五顏六色——當我為你帶來色彩繽紛的玩具時。

　　當我唱歌讓你跳舞時，我真的了解為什麼樹葉會有音樂，海浪為什麼會把各個聲部的合唱傳到大地傾聽的心海——當我唱歌讓你跳舞時。

　　當我把甜點放入你渴盼的雙手時，我終於明白為什麼花心裡有蜜，為什麼果實神祕地填滿蜜汁——當我把甜點放入你渴盼的雙手時。[9]

　　親愛的，當我親吻你的臉，逗你微笑的時候，我肯定

我了解晨光中的天空流洩著什麼樣的快樂，夏日微風帶給我什麼樣的愉悅——當我親吻你的臉、逗你微笑的時候。

WHEN I bring you coloured toys, my child, I understand why there is such a play of colours on clouds, on water, and why flowers are painted in tints-when I give coloured toys to you, my child.

When I sing to make you dance, I truly know why there is music in leaves, and why waves send their chorus of voices to the heart of the listening earth--when I sing to make you dance.

When I bring sweet things to your greedy hands, I know why there is honey in the cup of the flower, and why fruits are secretly filled with sweet juice--when I bring sweet things to your greedy hands.

When I kiss your face to make you smile, my darling, I surely understand what pleasure streams from the sky in morning light, and what delight the summer breeze brings to my body--when I kiss you to make you smile.

10

責罵

◆

DEFAMATION

孩子，為甚麼你眼中泛淚？

他們真壞，怎麼老是為了一點小事責罵你？

寫字的時候，你的手和臉沾了墨漬——就因為這樣他們罵你髒？

喔，呸！如果圓圓的月亮在臉上染上墨漬，他們膽敢罵月亮髒？

孩子，他們為了每一件細碎的瑣事責罵你，隨時都在挑你的小毛病。

你玩遊戲扯破了衣服——就因為這樣他們說你邋遢？

喔，呸！秋天的清晨在凌亂的碎雲堆中露出微笑，他們該怎麼說秋天的清晨呢？

孩子，別理會他們對你說的話。

孩子，別理會他們對你說的話。

他們把你的缺點列成長長的清單。大家都知道你多麼愛甜食——就因爲這樣他們說你貪？

喔，呸！我們是這麼地愛你，他們該怎麼說我們呢？

WHY are those tears in your eyes, my child? How horrid of them to be always scolding you for nothing?

You have stained your fingers and face with ink while writing — is that why they call you dirty?

O, fie! Would they dare to call the full moon dirty because it has smudged its face with ink?

For every little trifle they blame you, my child. They are ready to find fault for nothing.

You tore your clothes while playing--is that why they call you untidy?

O, fie! What would they call an autumn morning that smiles through its ragged clouds?

Take no heed of what they say to you, my child.

Take no heed of what they say to you, my child.

They make a long list of your misdeeds. Everybody knows how you love sweet things--is that why they call you greedy?

O, fie! What then would they call us who love you?

11

裁判

◆

THE JUDGE

你想怎麼說他就隨你吧，但我知道我的孩子的缺點。

我愛他，不是因為他有甚麼長處，而是因為他是我可愛的孩子。

如果你想方設法，只想估量他的功過，你怎麼可能知道他的可愛？

當我必須懲罰他時，他越發成為我存在的一部分。

當我讓他流下淚水，我的心也跟著他一起哭泣。

只有我能責罰他；只有付出愛的人，才有獎懲他人的權力。

SAY of him what you please, but I know my child's failings.

I do not love him because he is good, but because he is my little child.

How should you know how dear he can be when you try to weigh his merits against his faults?

When I must punish him he becomes all the more a part of my being.

When I cause his tears to come my heart weeps with him.

I alone have a right to blame and punish, for he only may chastise who loves.

12

玩具

◆

PLAYTHINGS

孩子，你是多麼快樂啊！一整個早上坐在沙塵地上，玩著掉落的樹枝。

我笑著看你把玩那小小的斷落的樹枝。

我忙著管理帳本，一小時又一小時地加總數字。

或許你會瞥我一眼，心想：「多蠢的遊戲啊，浪費你一整個早上的時間！」

孩子，現在我已經遺忘了沉醉在樹枝和泥餅中的本領了。

我追求昂貴的玩物，收集成堆成堆的金銀。

你不管找到甚麼，都能創造快樂的遊戲；我卻把時間和力氣全耗在追求我永遠得不到的東西。

我坐在脆弱的獨木舟裡，掙扎著渡過欲望之海，忘了我在玩的也是一場遊戲。

CHILD, how happy you are sitting in the dust, playing with a broken twig all the morning.

I smile at your play with that little bit of a broken twig.

I am busy with my accounts, adding up figures by the hour.

Perhaps you glance at me and think, "What a stupid game to spoil your morning with!"

Child, I have forgotten the art of being absorbed in sticks and mud-pies.

I seek out costly playthings, and gather lumps of gold and silver.

With whatever you find you create your glad games, I spend both my time and my strength over things I never can obtain.

In my frail canoe I struggle to cross the sea of desire, and forget that I too am playing a game.

13

天文學家

◆

THE ASTRONOMER

　我只不過說了：「晚上的時候，圓圓的滿月已纏陷在噶當樹枝裡，難道就沒人抓得到月亮嗎？」[10]

　可是葛格取笑我：「寶寶，我認識的小孩裡，你是最傻的一個。月亮離我們這麼遠，誰抓得到呢？」[11]

　我說：「葛格你真笨啊！媽媽探頭望向窗外，笑著看我們在屋外玩遊戲，你說她離我們很遠嗎？」

　他還是說：「你是個笨小孩！但是寶寶，你去哪裡找一張大網來網住月亮？」

　我說：「肯定你憑雙手就能抓住。」

　但是葛格笑著說：「我認識的小孩裡，你是最傻的一個。月亮如果近一些，你就知道月亮到底有多大了。」

我說：「葛格，學校到底教了你哪些亂七八糟的東西啊！媽媽低頭親吻我們的時候，你說她的臉看來很大嗎？」

但是葛格還是說：「你是個笨小孩。」

---

10. 噶當樹（Kadam），音譯卡鄧伯木（*Neolamarckia cadamba*），即大葉黃梁木或團花樹。卡鄧伯木是大喬木，結出的黃色團花呈圓球狀，有香氣。詩中小孩眼中所謂「圓圓的滿月」，可能就是噶當樹所結的黃色團花。
11. 根據原文的注解，dàdà 就是 brother（哥哥），或 brother 的兒語或暱稱；這裡參考中文口語，有時為了表示親暱，通常會把「哥哥」說成「葛格」，把「弟弟」說成「底迪」，因而把 dàdà 譯為「葛格」。

I ONLY said, "When in the evening the round full moon gets entangled among the branches of that *Kadam* tree, couldn't somebody catch it?"

But dâdâ [elder brother] laughed at me and said, "Baby, you are the silliest child I have ever known. The moon is ever so far from us, how could anybody catch it?"

I said, "Dâdâ how foolish you are! When mother looks out of her window and smiles down at us playing, would you call her far away?"

Still said, "You are a stupid child! But, baby, where could you find a net big enough to catch the moon with?"

I said, "Surely you could catch it with your hands."

But dâdâ laughed and said, "You are the silliest child I have known. If it came nearer, you would see how big the moon is."

I said, "Dâdâ, what nonsense they teach at your school! When mother bends her face down to kiss us does her face look very big?"

But still dâdâ says, "You are a stupid child."

14

雲朵和波浪

◆

CLOUDS AND WAVES

媽媽，住在雲上的人高聲呼喚我——

「我們一醒來就玩，一直玩到白天結束；

我們跟金色的黎明玩，我們跟銀色的月亮玩。」

我問：「可是我要怎樣才能上去你們那裡？」他們答：「你走到大地邊緣，朝天空舉起雙手，你就會被帶上雲間。」

我說：「媽媽在家裡等我。我怎能離開她，跟你們去呢？」

他們這時就微微一笑飄走了。

但是媽媽，我知道有個比登上雲間更好玩的遊戲。

我來作雲，妳來當月。

我用雙手遮住妳，我們家的屋頂就是藍天。

媽媽，住在海浪裡的人高聲呼喚我——

「我們從白天唱到黑夜；走啊走啊我們不斷旅行，根本不知道走過了哪些地方。」

我問：「可是我要怎樣才能加入你們？」他們答：「你走到海岸邊緣，站在岸邊緊閉雙眼，你就會被帶到波浪之間。」

我說：「媽媽總是要我晚上待在家裡——我怎能離開她，跟你們去呢？」

他們這時就微微一笑，跳著舞離開了。

但是媽媽，我知道有個比追波逐浪更好玩的遊戲。

我來作浪，妳來當奇特的海岸。

我笑著滾呀滾呀滾，滾倒在妳的膝上。

這世上不會有人知道我們倆身在何方。

MOTHER, the folk who live up in the clouds call out to me--

"We play from the time we wake till the day ends.

We play with the golden dawn, we play with the silver moon.

I ask, "But, how am I to get up to you?" They answer, "Come to the edge of the earth, lift up your hands to the sky, and you will be taken up into the clouds."

"My mother is waiting for me at home," I say. "How can I leave her and come?"

Then they smile and float away.

But I know a nicer game than that, mother.

I shall be the cloud and you the moon.

I shall cover you with both my hands, and our house-top will be the blue sky.

The folk who live in the waves call out to me--

"We sing from morning till night; on and on we travel and know not where we pass."

I ask, "But, how am I to join you?" They tell me, "Come to the edge of the shore and stand with your eyes tight shut, and you will be carried out upon the waves."

I say, "My mother always wants me at home in the evening--how can I leave her and go?"

Then they smile, dance and pass by.

But I know a better game than that.

I will be the waves and you will be a strange shore.

I shall roll on and on and on, and break upon your lap with laughter.

And no one in the world will know where we both are.

15

香巴花

◆

THE CHAMPA FLOWER

如果純粹出於好玩，我化成了一朵香巴花，站在那棵樹高高的枝上隨風搖曳歡笑，在剛剛萌芽的新葉上跳舞。媽媽，妳會認得我嗎？[12]

妳呼叫我：「寶貝，你在哪裡？」我會自己偷偷笑著，努力保持安靜。

我會悄悄張開花瓣，偷偷看妳在家裡忙著家務。

沐浴後，妳肩披著濕潤的髮，穿過香巴樹蔭，走向平日祈禱的小院；這時妳會聞到花香，只是妳不知道那香氣來自於我。

午餐後，妳坐在窗邊閱讀《羅摩衍那》，樹影落在妳

的髮上膝上；我會努力把我小小的影子投向妳的書頁，落在妳讀著的段落。[13]

只是妳猜得到那是妳的小寶貝投下的小小影子嗎？

到了夜裡，妳提燈走向牛棚。這時我會突然再次落回地面，再度化成妳的小孩，央求妳給我說個故事。

「你去哪了，你這頑皮的孩子？」

「不告訴妳，媽媽。」這將會是那時妳我之間的對話。

---

12. 香巴花（*champa* flower），又譯占婆花或金色花，亦即俗稱雞蛋花的緬梔（*Plumeria sp.*）。孟加拉和印度一帶的俗稱是「香巴花」，其英文拼音即 champa flower。香巴花的花瓣顏色很多，有白色、粉紅、桃紅色等，最常見的是花瓣基部呈金黃色，花瓣呈純白色的品種。緬梔源自於中南美洲，大航海時代之後，逐漸在南亞、東南亞等溫暖的地區廣為種植，作為園藝景觀植物。在孟加拉文化中，大部分白花都與死亡或葬禮有關，緬梔也不例外。

13. 《羅摩衍那》（*Ramayana*），意譯為《羅摩歷險記》，與《摩訶婆羅多》（*Mahābhārata*）並稱印度兩大長篇史詩。作者蟻蛭（Valmiki），全書七章，共計對句兩萬四千對。詩篇講述羅摩夫婦的故事。故事細節，請參考注 17。

S UPPOSING I became a *champa* flower, just for fun, and grew on a branch high up that tree, and shook in the wind with laughter and danced upon the newly budded leaves, would you know me, mother?

You would call, "Baby, where are you?" and I should laugh to myself and keep quite quiet.

I should slyly open my petals and watch you at your work.

When after your bath, with wet hair spread on your shoulders, you walked through the shadow of the *champa* tree to the little court where you say your prayers, you would notice the scent of the flower, but not know that it came from me.

When after the midday meal you sat at the window reading *Ramayana*, and the tree's shadow fell over your hair and your lap, I should fling my wee little shadow on to the page of your book, just where you were reading.

But would you guess that it was the tiny shadow of your little child?

When in the evening you went to the cow-shed with the lighted lamp in your hand, I should suddenly drop on to the earth again and be your own baby once more, and beg you to tell me a story.

"Where have you been, you naughty child?"

"I won't tell you, mother." That's what you and I would say then.

16

仙境

◆

FAIRYLAND

如果有人發現我的國王的宮殿，他的宮殿就會化為烏有。

銀白色的牆，閃閃發亮的金屋頂。

皇后住的宮殿有七座庭院，戴的珠寶價值七個王國的財富。

但是媽媽，讓我偷偷告訴妳國王的宮殿在哪裡。

他的宮殿就在我們的陽臺一角，就在那盆圖希花生長的地方。[14]

公主睡在遙遠的海岸，那裡有七座無法通行的海洋。

除了我，這個世間沒人找得到她。

她臂上戴著鐲子，耳際垂掛著珍珠耳環，長長的秀髮拂在地板上。

我的魔法棒一碰到她，她就會醒來；她微笑的時候，

唇間就會落下寶石。

但是媽媽，讓我在妳耳邊偷偷告訴妳：她就住在我們的陽臺一角，就在那盆圖希花生長的地方。

妳去河裡沐浴的時候，記得走上屋頂的那座陽臺。

我會坐在角落裡，就在牆影與牆影相遇的地方。

只有貓咪可以跟我一起上去，因為她知道故事中的理髮師住哪裡。

但是媽媽，讓我在妳耳邊偷偷告訴妳故事中的理髮師住哪裡。

他就住在我們的陽臺一角，就在那盆圖希花生長的地方。

---

14. 圖希花 (tulsi plant)，學名 *ocimum sanctum*，亦即聖羅勒（holy basil），是一種類似歐洲羅勒的香草，也是印度教毗濕奴派（Vaishnavites）教徒祭祀毗濕奴（Vishnu）的主要供品。如詩所述，這種香草經常種在方型高臺，放在家中或靠近祭祀的場所。在印度神話中，圖希花也被視為毗濕奴的妻子——吉祥天女（Lakshmi）的化身。吉祥天女專司幸福和財富。西印度古吉拉特邦（Gujarat）慶祝的排燈節，就是向吉祥天女表達敬意，祈求吉祥天女會為家庭帶來一整年的繁榮和富裕。

I F people came to know where my king's palace is, it would vanish into the air.

The walls are of white silver and the roof of shining gold.

The queen lives in a palace with seven courtyards, and she wears a jewel that cost all the wealth of seven kingdoms.

But let me tell you, mother, in a whisper, where my king's palace is.

It is at the corner of our terrace where the pot of the *tulsi* plant stands.

The princess lies sleeping on the far-away shore of the seven impassable seas.

There is none in the world who can find her but myself.

She has bracelets on her arms and pearl drops in her ears; her hair sweeps down upon the floor.

She will wake when I touch her with my magic wand, and jewels will fall from her lips when she smiles.

But let me whisper in your ear, mother; she is there in the corner of our terrace where the pot of the *tulsi* plant stands.

When it is time for you to go to the river for your bath, step up to that terrace on the roof.

I sit in the corner where the shadows of the walls meet together.

Only puss is allowed to come with me, for she knows where the barber in the story lives.

But let me whisper, mother, in your ear where the barber in the story lives.

It is at the corner of the terrace where the pot of the *tulsi* plant stands.

17

放逐之地

◆

THE LAND OF THE EXILE

　　媽媽，天上的日光已經漸漸變灰；不知道現在已經幾點了。

　　遊戲不再好玩了，所以我來找妳。今天是星期六，我們的假期。

　　媽媽，放下工作吧，來坐在窗邊，告訴我童話故事裡的特潘塔爾沙漠在哪裡？

　　雨的陰影徹頭徹尾遮蔽了白天。

　　狂暴的閃電伸出指甲，抓撓著天空。

　　當烏雲密佈、雷聲隆隆，我心裡覺得又害怕又歡喜，因為可以緊緊靠著妳。

　　大雨好幾個小時啪嗒啪嗒地打在竹葉上，陣風把窗戶刮得吱嘎吱嘎響。這時我喜歡獨自坐在房裡；媽媽，跟

妳坐在一起，聽妳說童話故事裡的特潘塔爾沙漠。

　　媽媽，那座沙漠在哪裡？在哪一座海的海岸？在哪座山的山腳？在哪位國王的國土？

　　那裡的田野沒有樹籬標記，沒有穿越田野的小徑讓村民在夜裡返回村落，或讓在森林收集乾柴的婦人揹著收穫到市集出售。

　　那裡的沙地有黃草數叢，僅有的一棵樹上住著一對睿智的老鳥——那裡就是特潘塔爾沙漠。

　　我可以想像在一個像這樣烏雲密佈的日子，年輕的王子騎著灰馬穿越沙漠，渡過陌生的水域去尋找被巨人關在宮殿裡的公主。

　　當雨霧從遙遠的天邊落下，當閃電劃過天際，宛如突然發作的疼痛，這時他是否會想起他那鬱鬱寡歡的母親？他那位遭受國王遺棄的母親正在一面清掃牛棚，一面拭淚？當他騎著馬，走過童話故事裡的特潘塔爾沙漠？

　　看啊，媽媽，白日雖未盡，天色已暗淡。外面的鄉村小路不見旅人蹤影。

　　牧童早已離開牧場回家；男人全都離開了田地，坐在茅屋簷下的毯子上，望著外面沉沉的烏雲。

媽媽，我已經把書本全部放回架上了──現在不要叫我做功課啊。

等我長大，長得跟爸爸一樣大的時候，我就會學會該學得的一切。

但是媽媽，就只有今天，請告訴我童話故事裡的特潘塔爾沙漠在哪裡？

MOTHER, the light has grown grey in the sky; I do not know what the time is.

There is no fun in my play, so I have come to you. It is Saturday, our holiday.

Leave off your work, mother; sit here by the window and tell me where the desert of Tepântar in the fairy tale is?

The shadow of the rains has covered the day from end to end.

The fierce lightning is scratching the sky with its nails.

When the clouds rumble and it thunders, I love to be afraid in my heart and cling to you.

When the heavy rain patters for hours on the bamboo leaves, and our windows shake and rattle at the gusts of wind, I like to sit alone in the room, mother, with you, and hear you talk about the desert of Tepântar in the fairy tale.

Where is it, mother, on the shore of what sea, at the foot of what hills, in the kingdom of what king?

There are no hedges there to mark the fields, no footpath across it by which the villagers reach their village in the evening, or the woman who gathers dry sticks in the forest can bring her load to the market. With patches of yellow grass in the sand and only one tree where the pair of wise old birds have their nest, lies the desert of Tepântar.

I can imagine how, on just such a cloudy day, the young son of the king is riding alone on a grey horse through the desert, in search of the princess who lies imprisoned in the giant's palace across that unknown water.

When the haze of the rain comes down in the distant sky, and lightning starts up like a sudden fit of pain, does he remember his unhappy mother, abandoned by the king, sweeping the cow-stall and wiping her eyes, while he rides through the desert of Tepântar in the fairy tale?

See, mother, it is almost dark before the day is over, and there are no travellers yonder on the village road.

The shepherd boy has gone home early from the pasture, and men have left their fields to sit on mats under the eaves of their huts, watching the scowling clouds.

Mother, I have left all my books on the shelf--do not ask me to do my lessons now.

When I grow up and am big like my father, I shall learn all that must be learnt.

But just for to-day, tell me, mother, where the desert of Tepântar in the fairy tale is?

18

雨天

◆

THE RAINY DAY

沉鬱的烏雲迅速聚攏在森林漆黑的邊緣。

孩子啊，不要出去！

湖邊那排棕櫚樹搖著頭，撞向陰沉的天；烏鴉斂起濕漉漉的翅膀，默默地棲息在羅望子樹上；河的東岸籠罩在越來越深的幽黯裡。

繫在圍籬的牛，大聲哞哞地叫。

孩子啊，你在這裡等著，等我把牛牽進牛欄。

男人擠在泛濫的田，捉著從溢水池中逃出來的魚；雨水在狹窄的小巷奔流，像故意從媽媽懷中逃開的男孩一直笑個不停。

聽啊，淺灘上有人正在高聲呼叫船夫。

孩子啊，日光黯淡，擺渡的渡口已經關閉。

天空似乎正隨著瘋狂傾瀉的雨迅速掉落；河裡的水轟轟作響，急急流去；女人在恆河邊汲滿了水，帶著水罐提早趕回家裡。

夜晚的燈，必須趕緊備好。

孩子啊，不要出去！

通往市集的路杳無人跡，通向河邊的小徑濕又滑。風呼呼地咆哮，不停地在竹林中奮力掙扎，猶如網中的困獸。

S ULLEN clouds are gathering fast over the black fringe of the forest.

O child, do not go out!

The palm trees in a row by the lake are smiting their heads against the dismal sky; the crows with their draggled wings are silent on the tamarind branches, and the eastern bank of the river is haunted by a deepening gloom.

Our cow is lowing loud, tied at the fence.

O child, wait here till I bring her into the stall.

Men have crowded into the flooded field to catch the fishes as they escape from the overflowing ponds; the rain water is running in rills through the narrow lanes like a laughing boy who has run away from his mother to tease her.

Listen, someone is shouting for the boatman at the ford.

O child, the daylight is dim, and the crossing at the ferry is closed.

The sky seems to ride fast upon the madly-rushing rain; the water in the river is loud and impatient; women have hastened home early from the Ganges with their filled pitchers.

The evening lamps must be made ready.

O child, do not go out!

The road to the market is desolate, the lane to the river is slippery. The wind is roaring and struggling among the bamboo branches like a wild beast tangled in a net.

19

紙船

◆

PAPER BOATS

日復一日，我把紙船一艘接一艘地放入奔流的溪。

在紙船上，我用又大又黑的字母寫下我和村落的名字。

我希望在某個異地他鄉，有人會發現紙船，知道我是誰。

我在船上裝滿了花園摘來的蘇麗花，希望這黎明之花會在夜晚抵達安全的國度。[15]

我把紙船放下水，抬頭看著天空——天上有小小的雲正拉起鼓漲的白帆。

我不知道是哪位玩伴派了雲船，從天上下來跟我的紙船競賽。

　　當黑夜來臨，我把臉埋入臂彎入睡，我夢見紙船在午夜的繁星之下漂流，不停地漂流。

　　睡眠仙子乘著我的紙船航行，船上載著祂們的夢，滿筐滿簍。

---

15. 蘇麗花（*shiuli* flowers）又名夜花，別名珊瑚茉莉（coral jasmine）。花極香，入夜開花，晨即閉合。

DAY by day I float my paper boats one by one down the running stream.

In big black letters I write my name on them and the name of the village where I live.

I hope that someone in some strange land will find them and know who I am.

I load my little boats with *shiuli* flowers from our garden, and hope that these blooms of the dawn will be carried safely to land in the night.

I launch my paper boats and look up into the sky and see the little clouds setting their white bulging sails.

I know not what playmate of mine in the sky sends them down the air to race with my boats!

When night comes I bury my face in my arms and dream that my paper boats float on and on under the midnight stars.

The fairies of sleep are sailing in them, and the lading is their baskets full of dreams.

20

水手

◆

THE SAILOR

船夫馬度把船停靠在拉傑根碼頭。

那船無用地堆滿了黃麻，已經無所事事地停在那裡好久好久。

如果他肯把船借我，我就給船裝上一百支槳，掛起船帆——五張、六張或七張。

我絕不把船駛入煩人的市集，我要航向仙界的七座海洋和十三條河。[16]

但是媽媽，妳不用坐在角落為我哭泣。

我不會像羅摩占陀羅[17]那樣走入森林，一去十四年才回來。

我要成為故事中的王子，我要在船上裝滿所有我喜歡的東西。

我要帶我的朋友亞述同行，我們會高高興興地航向仙界的七座海洋和十三條河。

我們會掛起船帆，在大清早的晨光中啓航。

正午時分，當妳在池塘沐浴的時候，我們已經航行到陌生國王的國土。

我們將駛過特普尼淺灘，把特潘塔爾沙漠丟在身後。

等我們回來，天色已經漸漸變暗，我會把我們的見聞全部告訴妳。

我要航向仙界的七座海洋和十三條河。

---

16. 從泰戈爾的一封寫於一八九一年的家書，這「七座海洋與十三條河」似乎與印度的創世神話有關，見 Alam F. & Chakravarty R.. (ed. 2011). *The Essential Tagore*. England: The Belknap Press of Harvard University Press， 頁 69。

17. 羅摩占陀羅，簡稱羅摩，是印度史詩《羅摩衍那》的主角，也是印度文化中的主要神祇。一般以為羅摩的本尊是濕婆神，即濕婆降生人間時的化身（Vishnu），也就是阿逾陀國（Ayodhya）的王子。阿逾陀國國王本擬傳位給羅摩，豈料遭遇羅摩繼母凱蔲的反對，只能另立凱蔲之子婆羅多（Bharata）為王。失去權勢的羅摩遭到放逐，於是便偕同妻子悉妲（Sita）、弟弟拉斯曼（Shri Lakshmana）向南走到丹達卡森林（Dandaka），一去十四年。

THE boat of the boatman Madhu is moored at the wharf of Rajgunj.

It is uselessly laden with jute, and has been lying there idle for ever so long.

If he would only lend me his boat, I should man her with a hundred oars, and hoist sails, five or six or seven.

I should never steer her to stupid markets. I should sail the seven seas and the thirteen rivers of fairyland.

But, mother, you won't weep for me in a corner.

I am not going into the forest like Ramachandra to come back only after fourteen years.

I shall become the prince of the story, and fill my boat with whatever I like.

I shall take my friend Ashu with me. We shall sail merrily across the seven seas and the thirteen rivers of fairyland.

We shall set sail in the early morning light.

When at noontide you are bathing at the pond, we shall be in the land of a strange king.

We shall pass the ford of Tirpurni, and leave behind us the desert of Tepântar.

When we come back it will be getting dark, and I shall tell you of all that we have seen.

I shall cross the seven seas and the thirteen rivers of fairyland.

21

更遠的河岸

◆

THE FURTHER BANK

我渴望到那裡去，到更遠的那座河岸。

在那裡，船隻綁在竹竿上，排成一行行；

在那裡，男人一早坐船渡河，扛著犁到遙遠的田地耕作。

在那裡，牧童催著低聲哞叫的牛，讓牠們渡河到岸邊的草地上吃草。

到了夜裡，他們全都回家了，只有狼群在野草叢生的島上嚎叫。

媽媽，如果妳不介意，我長大後想在渡頭當一名船伕。

他們說高高的河岸後面藏有許多奇異的池塘。

雨季過後，野鴨成群飛到那裡聚會；濃密的蘆葦繞著池邊生長，蘆葦叢中有許多水鳥正在生蛋。

在那裡，舞著尾巴的鷸把小小的足跡印上乾淨的軟泥；

在那裡，開著白花的長草到了夜裡就邀請月光在草浪上蕩漾。

媽媽，如果妳不介意，我長大後想在渡頭當一名船伕。

我要從河的這岸渡到彼岸；村裡所有男孩女孩在河中沐浴時，看到我都會覺得讚嘆。

當太陽爬上中天，當早晨漸漸變成正午，我會跑回來對妳說：「媽媽，我餓了！」

當白天結束，當影子紛紛退回樹下，我會在薄暮之中回家。

我絕不會像爸爸那樣離開妳，離開妳到城裡工作。

媽媽，如果妳不介意，我長大後想在渡頭當一名船伕。

I LONG to go over there to the further bank of the river,
Where those boats are tied to the bamboo poles in a line;

Where men cross over in their boats in the morning with ploughs on their shoulders to till their far-away fields;

Where the cowherds make their lowing cattle swim across to the riverside pasture;

Whence they all come back home in the evening, leaving the jackals to howl in the island overgrown with weeds,

Mother, if you don't mind, I should like to become the boatman of the ferry when I am grown up.

They say there are strange pools hidden behind that high bank,

Where flocks of wild ducks come when the rains are over, and thick reeds grow round the margins where waterbirds lay their eggs;

Where snipes with their dancing tails stamp their tiny footprints upon the clean soft mud;

Where in the evening the tall grasses crested with white flowers invite the moonbeam to float upon their waves.

Mother, if you don't mind, I should like to become the boatman of the ferryboat when I am grown up.

I shall cross and cross back from bank to bank, and all the boys and girls of the village will wonder at me while they are bathing.

When the sun climbs the mid sky and morning wears on to noon, I shall come running to you, saying, "Mother, I am hungry!"

When the day is done and the shadows cower under the trees, I shall come back in the dusk.

I shall never go away from you into the town to work like father.

Mother, if you don't mind, I should like to become the boatman of the ferryboat when I am grown up.

22

花的學校

◆

THE FLOWER-SCHOOL

　　暴風雨在天上的雲層之間隆隆作響，六月的雨一陣陣落下。

　　濕潤的東風吹過低矮的灌木叢，來到竹林間吹奏風笛。

　　有一群草花突然從不爲人知的地方冒出來，在草地上樂瘋了似地跳舞。

　　媽媽，我眞的覺得這群草花是到地底的學校上學。

　　她們關著門寫功課；如果時間還沒到她們就想出來玩，老師會叫她們到角落罰站。

　　但是雨季一來，她們就放假了。

　　森林裡的樹枝相互碰撞，樹葉在野風裡沙沙作響，閃電雲拍著巨大的手——就在這時，花孩子紛紛跑了出來，穿著粉紅色、黃色和白色的衣裳。

　　媽媽，妳知道嗎？花孩子的家就在天上，就在星星的

家鄉。

　　妳難道沒看到她們是多麼急著要去那裡嗎？妳難道不知道她們為甚麼那麼匆忙嗎？

　　當然我可以猜到她們是對誰伸出雙臂：她們有她們自己的媽媽，就像我一樣。

WHEN storm clouds rumble in the sky and June showers come down,

The moist east wind comes marching over the heath to blow its bagpipes among the bamboos.

Then crowds of flowers come out of a sudden, from nobody knows where, and dance upon the grass in wild glee.

Mother, I really think the flowers go to school underground.

They do their lessons with doors shut, and if they want to come out to play before it is time, their master makes them stand in a corner.

When the rains come they have their holidays.

Branches clash together in the forest, and the leaves rustle in the wild wind, the thunder-clouds clap their giant hands and the flower children rush out in dresses of pink and yellow and white.

Do you know, mother, their home is in the sky, where the stars are.

Haven't you seen how eager they are to get there? Don't you know why they are in such a hurry?

Of course, I can guess to whom they raise their arms: they have their mother as I have my own.

23

商人

◆

THE MERCHANT

媽媽，想像妳留在家裡，我去陌生的國度旅行。

想像我的船已靠在碼頭，而且已經裝滿了行李。

媽媽，妳現在先想好，再告訴我妳希望我爲妳帶什麼禮物回來。

媽媽，妳想要成堆成堆的金子嗎？

就在那裡，金河兩岸的田野長滿了金色作物。

就在那裡，金色的香巴花在森林小路落了一地。[18]

我要收集所有的金色作物和香巴花，裝滿好幾百個籃子。

媽媽，妳想要珍珠嗎？大如秋天雨滴的珍珠？

我要航行到珍珠島沿岸。就在那裡，就在晨光之中，珍珠顫動在草地上的花朵之間，珍珠掉落在草地上，珍

珠在洶湧的浪花裡灑落沙灘。

　　我要送哥哥一對生有雙翼的馬，讓他在雲間翱翔。

　　我要送爸爸一枝魔法筆；在他不知不覺之間，魔法筆就自動幫他把書寫好。

　　媽媽，至於妳，我一定會爲妳找到那盒價值七座國土的珠寶。

----

18. 香巴花，參看注 12。

IMAGINE, mother, that you are to stay at home and I am to travel into strange lands.

Imagine that my boat is ready at the landing fully laden.

Now think well, mother, before you say what I shall bring for you when I come back.

Mother, do you want heaps and heaps of gold?

There, by the banks of golden streams, fields are full of golden harvest.

And in the shade of the forest path the golden *champa* flowers drop on the ground.

I will gather them all for you in many hundred baskets.

Mother, do you want pearls big as the raindrops of autumn?

I shall cross to the pearl island shore. There in the early morning light pearls tremble on the meadow flowers, pearls drop on the grass, and pearls are scattered on the sand in spray by the wild sea-waves.

My brother shall have a pair of horses with wings to fly among the clouds.

For father I shall bring a magic pen that, without his knowing, will write of itself.

For you, mother, I must have the casket and jewel that cost seven kings their kingdoms.

24

同情

◆

SYMPATHY

親愛的媽媽，如果我只是一隻小狗，不是妳的寶貝，如果我想吃妳盤中的食物，妳會對我說「不行」嗎？

妳會跟我說：「走開！你這頑皮的小狗！」然後把我趕走嗎？

那麼走吧，媽媽妳走吧！妳叫我的時候，我永遠不會走向妳，我永遠不會再讓妳餵我吃飯。

親愛的媽媽，如果我只是一隻小小的綠鸚鵡，不是妳的寶貝，妳會把我鎖起來，不讓我飛走嗎？

妳會搖著指頭對我說：「真是一隻討人厭的小鳥！怎麼日夜都在啃咬鐵鍊？」

那麼走吧，媽媽妳走吧！我要跑進森林，永遠不會再讓妳抱我在懷裡。

I F I were only a little puppy, not your baby, mother dear, would you say "No" to me if I tried to eat from your dish?

Would you drive me off, saying to me, "Get away, you naughty little puppy?"

Then go, mother, go! I will never come to you when you call me, and never let you feed me any more.

If I were only a little green parrot, and not your baby, mother dear, would you keep me chained lest I should fly away?

Would you shake your finger at me and say, "What an ungrateful wretch of a bird! It is gnawing at its chain day and night?"

Then, go, mother, go! I will run away into the woods; I will never let you take me in your arms again.

25

理想的工作

◆

VOCATION

早上鐘敲十響的時候，我沿著我們家的巷子走路去上學。

每天我都碰到小販在叫賣：「手環，水晶手環啊！」

他沒有一定得趕快做完的事，沒有一定得走的路，沒有一定得去的地方，沒有必須回家的時間。

我真希望我是個小販，一整天在街上叫賣：「手環，水晶手環啊！」

下午四點，我從學校走路回家。

透過花園的鏤空大門，我看到那戶人家的園丁正在挖土。

他拿著鏟子，想做什麼就做什麼；他的衣服沾滿泥土，如果他曬多了或淋濕了，沒有人會來帶他去梳洗。

我真希望我是個園丁，一整天待在園中挖土，沒有人

會來責罵勸阻。

晚上天才剛剛黑下來，媽媽就要我上床睡覺。

透過臥室開著的窗，我看到守夜人在街上走來走去。

巷子又暗又冷清；街燈豎立，宛如頭上長了一顆紅眼睛的巨人。

守夜人搖著燈籠，走在他的影子旁邊，一生一世都不用上床睡覺。

我真希望我是個守夜人，整夜走在街上，提著燈籠追逐一個個影子。

WHEN the gong sounds ten in the morning and I walk to school by our lane,

Every day I meet the hawker crying, "Bangles, crystal bangles!"

There is nothing to hurry him on, there is no road he must take, no place he must go to, no time when he must come home.

I wish I were a hawker, spending my day in the road, crying, "Bangles, crystal bangles!"

When at four in the afternoon I come back from the school,

I can see through the gate of that house the gardener digging the ground.

He does what he likes with his spade, he soils his clothes with dust, nobody takes him to task if he gets baked in the sun or gets wet.

I wish I were a gardener digging away at the garden with nobody to stop me from digging.

Just as it gets dark in the evening and my mother sends me to bed,

I can see through my open window the watchman walking up and down.

The lane is dark and lonely, and the street-lamp stands like a giant with one red eye in its head.

The watchman swings his lantern and walks with his shadow at his side, and never once goes to bed in his life.

I wish I were a watchman walking the streets all night, chasing the shadows with my lantern.

26

哥哥

◆

SUPERIOR

媽媽，妳的寶寶眞傻！她眞是太孩子氣太可笑了！
她分不清街上的燈和星星的光。

我們用來玩吃飯遊戲的小石頭，她竟以爲那是眞的食
物，竟想把那石頭放進嘴裡。

我打開一本書放在她面前，要她學習 abc；她竟把書撕
了，還無緣無故地開心大叫。這就是妳的寶寶的學習方
式。

每當我搖著頭，生氣地罵她太頑皮，她卻笑了，以爲
那是一件超有趣的事。

大家都知道爸爸不在家，但是如果我在遊戲之中叫了

一聲「爸爸」，她卻以為爸爸就在近處，興奮地到處張望。

我給洗衣工人用來運送衣服的驢子上課時，我都交代她要叫我「老師」，但是她卻無緣無故地大聲叫我「葛格」。[19]

妳的寶寶還想捉住月亮呢。她真的好好笑，她把象神說成「匠神」。[20]
媽媽，妳的寶寶真傻！她真是太孩子氣太可笑了！

---

19. 兒語 dâdâ，原文的注解是「哥哥」（elder brother）。這裡之所以會翻譯成「葛格」，理由見本書注 11。

20. 根據原文的注解：Ganesh 是個很普通的印度名字，也是象頭神的名字。這個名字通常翻譯成「甘尼許」，不過詩裡的小女孩發錯了兩個母音，念成了「嘎奴許」（Gânush）。誠如原文注解所說，甘尼許也是印度常見神祇象神的名字。象神是濕婆（Shiva）和雪山神女帕爾瓦蒂（Parvati）的兒子，象徵好運和財富，具有御軍和傳播知識的能力。象神也是印度文藝工作者或學生最常祈禱的神，希望象神掃除一切障礙，幫助他們邁向成功。這裡的小女孩把象神的名字念錯，這在她哥哥眼裡是一件愚蠢的事，暗示小女孩的學習能力有待加強。配合詩中敘述者的口吻與象神在學生心目中的地位，譯者捨棄音譯，選擇把 Ganesh 譯為「象神」，而 Ganesh 的錯誤發音 Gânush 則配合「象神」，譯「匠神」。關於象神的參考資料，參見貓頭鷹出版社製作：《追尋印度史詩之美：100 個神話故事全圖解》，頁 78-79。

MOTHER, your baby is silly! She is so absurdly childish!

She does not know the difference between the lights in the streets and the stars.

When we play at eating with pebbles, she thinks they are real food, and tries to put them into her mouth.

When I open a book before her and ask her to learn her a, b, c, she tears the leaves with her hands and roars for joy at nothing; this is your baby's way of doing her lesson.

When I shake my head at her in anger and scold her and call her naughty, she laughs and thinks it great fun.

Everybody knows that father is away, but if in play I call aloud "Father," she looks about her in excitement and thinks that father is near.

When I hold my class with the donkeys that our washerman brings to carry away the clothes and I warn her that I am the schoolmaster, she will scream for no reason and call me dâdâ.

Your baby wants to catch the moon. She is so funny; she calls Ganesh Gânush.

Mother, your baby is silly, she is so absurdly childish!

27

小大人

◆

THE LITTLE BIG MAN

　我的個子小，因為我是小小孩。等我長到像爸爸一樣的年紀，我就會變高。

　老師走過來說：「時間不早了，去把你的寫字板和書拿過來。」

　我會跟他說：「你不知道我已經像我爸爸一樣大了嗎？我不用再寫功課了。」

　老師會很驚奇地說：「如果他想放下書本就放下書本，因為他是個大人。」

　我會自己穿好衣服，走向人潮擁擠的市集。

　叔叔會衝過來說：「孩子，你會走丟的，讓我抱著你。」

　我會跟叔叔說：「叔叔，你沒看到嗎？我已經像我爸爸一樣大了。我一定要自己去市集。」

　叔叔會說：「是的，他想去哪兒就去哪兒，因為他是

個大人。」

　　媽媽沐浴回來看到我正在付錢給奶媽，因為我知道怎
麼用鑰匙打開放錢的盒子。

　　媽媽會說：「頑皮的孩子，你在做甚麼呀？」

　　我會告訴她：「媽媽，妳不知道嗎？我已經像爸爸一
樣大了，我一定要自己付錢給奶媽。」

　　媽媽會自言自語地說：「他想把錢給誰就給誰，因為
他是個大人。」

　　十月放假的時候，爸爸就回家了。他以為我還是小寶
寶，從城裡給我帶來小鞋子和小小的絲質長袍。

　　我會對他說：「爸爸，這些東西送給葛格吧，因為我
已經像你一樣大了。」

　　爸爸會想一下說：「他想買甚麼衣服就自己去買，因
為他是個大人。」

I AM small because I am a little child. I shall be big when I am as old as my father is.

My teacher will come and say, "It is late, bring your slate and your books."

I shall tell him, "Do you not know I am as big as father? And I must not have lessons any more."

My master will wonder and say, "He can leave his books if he likes, for he is grown up."

I shall dress myself and walk to the fair where the crowd is thick.

My uncle will come rushing up to me and say, "You will get lost, my boy; let me carry you."

I shall answer, "Can't you see, uncle, I am as big as father. I must go to the fair alone."

Uncle will say, "Yes, he can go wherever he likes, for he is grown up."

Mother will come from her bath when I am giving money to my nurse, for I shall know how to open the box with my key.

Mother will say, "What are you about, naughty child?"

I shall tell her, "Mother, don't you know, I am as big as father, and I must give silver to my nurse."

Mother will say to herself, "He can give money to whom he

likes, for he is grown up."

In the holiday time in October father will come home and, thinking that I am still a baby, will bring for me from the town little shoes and small silken frocks.

I shall say, "Father, give them to my dâdâ , for I am as big as you are."

Father will think and say, "He can buy his own clothes if he likes, for he is grown up."

28

十二點

◆

TWELVE O'CLOCK

媽媽，我現在真的很想放下功課，我已經讀了一整個早上的書了。

妳說現在才十二點。假設現在時間真的還早，假設現在才只是中午十二點，但是妳難道就不能想像現在已經是下午了嗎？

我很容易就能想像太陽現在已經落入稻田邊，還有那位老漁婦正在池邊採集做晚餐的香草。

我只要閉上眼睛，就能想像瑪達樹下的陰影越來越暗，池塘裡的水變得又黑又亮。

如果十二點可以在夜晚降臨，爲甚麼夜晚不能在十二點降臨？

MOTHER, I do want to leave off my lessons now. I have been at my book all the morning.

You say it is only twelve o'clock. Suppose it isn't any later; can't you ever think it is afternoon when it is only twelve o'clock?

I can easily imagine now that the sun has reached the edge of that rice-field, and the old fisher-woman is gathering herbs for her supper by the side of the pond.

I can just shut my eyes and think that the shadows are growing darker under the *madar* tree, and the water in the pond looks shiny black.

If twelve o'clock can come in the night, why can't the night come when it is twelve o'clock?

29

作者

◆

AUTHORSHIP

妳說爸爸寫了很多書，可是他寫的書我都看不懂。

他一整晚都在讀書給妳聽，可是妳眞的聽懂他的意思嗎？

媽媽，妳給我們說的故事多好聽呀！我就不懂爸爸爲甚麼不能寫那樣的故事？

難道他自己的媽媽從來不曾跟他說過巨人、仙子和公主的故事嗎？

難道他現在把那些故事全都忘了？

他時常錯過洗澡的時間，妳得要走去叫他一百次。

妳得等他，幫他把飯菜保溫，可是他卻老是一直寫寫寫，一直忘忘忘。

爸爸老是在玩寫書的遊戲。

如果我去爸爸的房裡玩，妳就走來罵我：「你這孩子真頑皮！」

如果我發出最小的聲音，妳就會說：「你沒看到爸爸在工作嗎？」

老是寫了又寫，寫了又寫——這遊戲到底有甚麼樂趣？

如果我拿爸爸的鋼筆或鉛筆，像他那樣在書上寫 a, b, c, d, e, f, g, h, i ——媽媽，妳為甚麼對我發脾氣了？

爸爸寫字的時候，妳一句話也沒說呀。

爸爸浪費了那麼一大疊紙，妳似乎一點也不介意。

只要我拿一張紙來摺紙船，妳就會說：「孩子，你真是個煩人精呀！」

爸爸浪費了一張又一張紙，還在紙的兩面畫滿黑色的記號——這妳要怎麼說呢？

YOU say that father writes a lot of books, but what he writes I don't understand.

He was reading to you all the evening, but could you really make out what he meant?

What nice stories, mother, you can tell us! Why can't father write like that, I wonder?

Did he never hear from his own mother stories of giants and fairies and princesses?

Has he forgotten them all?

Often when he gets late for his bath you have to go and call him an hundred times.

You wait and keep his dishes warm for him, but he goes on writing and forgets.

Father always plays at making books.

If ever I go to play in father's room, you come and call me, "what a naughty child!"

If I make the slightest noise, you say, "Don't you see that father's at his work?"

What's the fun of always writing and writing?

When I take up father's pen or pencil and write upon his book just as he does,--a, b, c, d, e, f, g, h, i,--why do you get cross with me, then, mother?

You never say a word when father writes.

When my father wastes such heaps of paper, mother, you don't seem to mind at all.

But if I take only one sheet to make a boat with, you say, "Child, how troublesome you are!"

What do you think of father's spoiling sheets and sheets of paper with black marks all over on both sides?

30

壞郵差

◆

THE WICKED POSTMAN

親愛的媽媽，妳爲甚麼坐在地板上，那麼安靜又那麼沉默？

雨點從開著的窗飄進來，把妳全淋濕了，妳卻不在意。

妳聽到鐘敲四響嗎？哥哥就要放學回家了。

到底發生了甚麼事？妳看起來好奇怪。

今天——妳沒收到爸爸寄來的信嗎？

我看到郵差揹著郵袋，幾乎給鎮上所有人都送了信。

只有爸爸的信，他要留著自己讀。

我確定這個郵差是個大壞蛋。

但是親愛的媽媽，妳不要爲這件事難過。

明天——隔壁村裡有個市集，妳派女傭去那裡買些紙筆。

我自己來寫爸爸所有的信；妳不會在信裡找到任何錯誤。

　　我會從 A 開始寫起，一直寫到 K。

　　可是媽媽，妳爲甚麼笑了？

　　妳不相信我可以寫得像爸爸那麼好是嗎？

　　我會在紙上好好地畫分隔線，我會把所有字母寫得又大又漂亮。

　　等我寫完，妳以爲我會像爸爸那麼笨？竟把信投進壞郵差的袋子裡？

　　我會親自把信送到妳手上，一刻也不耽擱，而且我會一個字母一個字母讀給妳聽。

　　我知道眞正好看的信，郵差是不會送來給妳讀的。

WHY do you sit there on the floor so quiet and silent, tell me, mother dear?

The rain is coming in through the open window, making you all wet, and you don't mind it.

Do you hear the gong striking four? It is time for my brother to come home from school.

What has happened to you that you look so strange?

Haven't you got a letter from father to-day?

I saw the postman bringing letters in his bag for almost everybody in the town.

Only, father's letters he keeps to read himself. I am sure the postman is a wicked man.

But don't be unhappy about that, mother dear.

To-morrow is market day in the next village. You ask your maid to buy some pens and papers.

I myself will write all father's letters; you will not find a single mistake.

I shall write from A right up to K.

But, mother, why do you smile?

You don't believe that I can write as nicely as father does!

But I shall rule my paper carefully, and write all the letters beautifully big.

When I finish my writing, do you think I shall be so foolish as father and drop it into the horrid postman's bag?

I shall bring it to you myself without waiting, and letter by letter help you to read my writing.

I know the postman does not like to give you the really nice letters.

31

英雄

◆

THE HERO

媽媽，想像我們在一個又陌生又危險的國度旅行。

妳坐在轎子裡，我騎著紅馬，小跑步地跟在妳身邊。

黃昏時刻，太陽已經下山。佐拉迪祁荒原在我們眼前展開，看來又慘白又灰暗。大地一片孤寂，寸草不生。

妳嚇壞了，心裡想：「真不知我們來到甚麼地方！」

我對妳說：「媽媽，別怕。」

地上長滿了釘子似刺人的草，一條窄窄的，時隱時現的小路從草地中間穿過。

遠處寬闊的田野看不到牛群——牠們已經全部回到村裡的牛欄。

大地和天空漸漸暗下來，四周的景物漸漸模糊，我們看不清自己正走向何處。

妳突然叫住我，低聲問道：「那火光，靠近河岸的那道火光是甚麼？」

就在那時，四周突然爆出一陣可怕的叫喊，許多人影朝著我們衝來。

妳坐在轎子裡，縮成一團；妳不斷祈禱，不斷呼喚衆神的名字，一遍又一遍。

轎夫嚇得發抖，紛紛跑去荊棘叢裡躲藏。

我大聲對妳說：「媽媽別害怕，有我在。」

那群壞蛋拿著長棍，披著狂亂的散髮，越跑越靠近我們。

我對他們喊道：「注意了，你們這群壞蛋！再靠近一步，你們就死定了。」

他們再度發出一陣可怕的叫喊，迅速朝我們衝來。

妳緊抓著我的手說：「親愛的孩子，看在老天的份上，快去躲起來吧。」

我回答道：「媽媽別擔心，看我的。」

於是我一踩馬鐙，策馬向前衝過去；我的劍和盾相互撞擊，鏗鏘作響。

媽媽，這場戰鬥實在太激烈了。如果妳從轎子往外看一眼，一定會嚇得直打冷顫。

大多數壞蛋飛快地逃走了，但有更多的壞蛋被斬成了碎片。

我知道妳坐在轎子裡，一定以爲妳兒子這時已經死了。

但我血跡斑斑地走向妳，對妳說：「媽媽，戰鬥結束了。」

妳從轎子裡走出來，親吻著我，把我擁入懷裡，自言自語地說：「如果沒有兒子保護我，真的不知道該怎麼辦才好。」

　　生活一天過一天，每天都有一千件無用的事發生，爲甚麼就不能偶爾發生一次這樣的事？

　　就像發生在故事書裡的事。

　　哥哥會說：「這可能嗎？我一直覺得他很瘦弱！」

　　所有村人都會很驚奇地說：「他的母親眞是幸運啊！那男孩當時就在她身邊。」

M OTHER, let us imagine we are travelling, and passing through a strange and dangerous country.

You are riding in a palanquin and I am trotting by you on a red horse.

It is evening and the sun goes down. The waste of *Joradighi* lies wan and grey before us. The land is desolate and barren.

You are frightened and thinking--"I know not where we have come to."

I say to you, "Mother, do not be afraid."

The meadow is prickly with spiky grass, and through it runs a narrow broken path.

There are no cattle to be seen in the wide field; they have gone to their village stalls.

It grows dark and dim on the land and sky, and we cannot tell where we are going.

Suddenly you call me and ask me in a whisper, "What light is that near the bank?"

Just then there bursts out a fearful yell, and figures come running towards us.

You sit crouched in your palanquin and repeat the names of the gods in prayer.

The bearers, shaking in terror, hide themselves in the thorny bush.

I shout to you, "Don't be afraid, mother. I am here."

With long sticks in their hands and hair all wild about their heads, they come nearer and nearer.

I shout, "Have a care! you villains! One step more and you are dead men."

They give another terrible yell and rush forward.

You clutch my hand and say, "Dear boy, for heaven's sake, keep away from them."

I say, "Mother, just you watch me."

Then I spur my horse for a wild gallop, and my sword and buckler clash against each other.

The fight becomes so fearful, mother, that it would give you a cold shudder could you see it from your palanquin.

Many of them fly, and a great number are cut to pieces.

I know you are thinking, sitting all by yourself, that your boy must be dead by this time.

But I come to you all stained with blood, and say, "Mother, the fight is over now."

You come out and kiss me, pressing me to your heart, and you say to yourself,

"I don't know what I should do if I hadn't my boy to escort me."

A thousand useless things happen day after day, and why couldn't such a thing come true by chance?

It would be like a story in a book.

My brother would say, "Is it possible? I always thought he was so delicate!"

Our village people would all say in amazement, "Was it not lucky that the boy was with his mother?"

32

告別

◆

THE END

離開的時候到了；媽媽，我走了。

清冷的黎明，灰濛濛的時刻，妳伸出雙臂想擁抱床上的寶貝，這時我會說：「寶貝不在了！」媽媽，我走了。

我會化成一縷輕風吹拂著妳；妳到河裡沐浴時，我會化作漣漪，一遍又一遍地親吻妳。

起風的夜晚，雨點滴答滴答地落在葉片上，妳會聽到我在妳床邊低語，我的笑聲會隨著閃電，透過洞開的窗戶閃入妳房裡。

如果妳躺著睡不著，想著妳的寶貝直到夜深，我會從星星那裡對妳歌唱：「睡吧，媽媽睡吧。」

我將隨著游移的月光，悄悄地移上妳的床，在妳入睡的時候，躺臥在妳胸前。

　　我將化成一個夢，透過妳微張的眼皮潛入妳的睡眠深處；當妳醒來，驚異地望向四周，我會迅速遁入黑暗，像一隻閃爍的螢火蟲。

　　熱鬧的十勝節 [21] 裡，鄰居的孩子會來我們家玩，我將融入笛子的樂音，在妳心頭迴盪一整天。

　　親愛的阿姨帶著十勝節禮物來訪，她會問妳：「妹妹，我們的寶貝在哪裡？」妳會輕輕地告訴她：「他在我的瞳仁裡，他在我的身體裡，他在我的靈魂裡。」

---

21. 十勝節（puja），音譯「普迦」，是印度教、耆那教、佛教、錫克教等各宗派信徒的祭神儀式。普迦可分為大型寺院慶典、小型日常家庭祝禱，以及在野外樹林、河流或任何神聖場所舉行的祭儀。寺院慶典由祭司負責數十、甚至六十多個步驟的繁複儀軌，最為隆重。著名的普迦有九夜節（Navaratri）、妙音天女節（Saraswati Puja）、杜爾迦女神節（Durga Puja）、象神節（Ganesh Chaturthi）等。家中設有神龕的家庭，也可日日進行奉拜。常見的祭品有香、花、水果、樹葉、水和糖果等。

I T is time for me to go, mother; I am going.

When in the paling darkness of the lonely dawn you stretch out your arms for your baby in the bed, I shall say, "Baby is not there!"--mother, I am going.

I shall become a delicate draught of air and caress you; and I shall be ripples in the water when you bathe, and kiss you and kiss you again.

In the gusty night when the rain patters on the leaves you will hear my whisper in your bed, and my laughter will flash with the lightning through the open window into your room.

If you lie awake, thinking of your baby till late into the night, I shall sing to you from the stars, "Sleep mother, sleep."

On the straying moonbeams I shall steal over your bed, and lie upon your bosom while you sleep.

I shall become a dream, and through the little opening of your eyelids I shall slip into the depths of your sleep; and when you wake up and look round startled, like a twinkling firefly I shall flit out into the darkness.

When, on the great festival of *puja*, the neighbours' children come and play about the house, I shall melt into the music of the flute and throb in your heart all day.

Dear auntie will come with *puja*-presents and will ask, "Where is our baby, sister?" Mother, you will tell her softly, "He is in the pupils of my eyes, he is in my body and in my soul."

33

召喚

◆

THE RECALL

她離開的時候，夜很黑。他們都睡了。

此時夜很黑，我召喚她：「回來吧，親愛的。世界已經入睡；星星此刻正在相互對望，如果妳回來一會，不會有人知道的。」

她離開的時候，花樹正含苞，春天正年輕。

此時繁花盛開，春天正好，我召喚她：「回來吧，親愛的。孩童正玩得起勁，他們隨手採花又隨手拋撒。如果妳回來帶走一朵小花，不會有人介意的。」

那些在昔日玩鬧的人，依然還在玩鬧，依然還在揮霍生命。

聽著他們的叨叨絮語，我召喚她：「回來吧，親愛的。媽媽心裡滿溢著愛，如果妳只是回來向媽媽討一個親親，不會有人妒恨的。」

THE night was dark when she went away, and they slept.

The night is dark now, and I call for her, "Come back, my darling; the world is asleep; and no one would know, if you came for a moment while stars are gazing at stars."

She went away when the trees were in bud and the spring was young.

Now the flowers are in high bloom and I call, "Come back, my darling. The children gather and scatter flowers in reckless sport. And if you come and take one little blossom no one will miss it."

Those that used to play are playing still, so spendthrift is life.

I listen to their chatter and call, "Come back, my darling, for mother's heart is full to the brim with love, and if you come to snatch only one little kiss from her no one will grudge it."

34

最初的茉莉

◆

THE FIRST JASMINES

啊，茉莉花，白色的茉莉花！[22]
我依稀記得第一次手捧滿滿的茉莉，白色的茉莉。

向來我就愛陽光，天空和綠色的大地。
向來我就愛聽河水流過黑夜的淙淙低語。
在寂寥的荒野裡，秋天的夕陽在小路的轉彎處迎面朝我走來，宛如新娘揭開面紗迎向情人。
只是當我想起兒時第一次手捧白色的茉莉，心裡依舊感到甜蜜。

我曾有許多快樂的日子，我曾與許多歡樂的人共同度過節慶之夜。
多少個下著雨、灰濛濛的清晨，我曾低吟一首又一首沒有意義的歌。

許多夜裡我曾戴上愛之手編織的巴古拉斯花環。

只是當我想起兒時第一次手捧新鮮的茉莉，心裡依舊感到甜蜜。

---

22. 茉莉的英文名字 "jasmine" 來自波斯語 "yasmin"，意指「來自神的禮物」。茉莉的種類多達 200 種，是歐亞大陸、大洋洲熱帶與副熱帶本土植物。茉莉在南亞廣為種植，無論公共庭園或私人宅院中皆可見到。在這些地區，茉莉花常被製作成頭飾，在婚禮、宗教儀式與慶典等場合佩戴。祭神的供品也會用到茉莉花，例如供奉哈努曼（Hanuman）時，供品之中就必須包含茉莉花。在印度教裡，茉莉代表純潔，是毗濕奴（Vishnu）的象徵符號。泰戈爾的詩常寫到茉莉，例如《漂鳥集》的第 237 首即是。這裡敘述者提到第一次手捧白色茉莉的甜蜜回憶，應該是指參與祭神慶典的經驗。

AH, these jasmines, these white jasmines!
I seem to remember the first day when I filled my
hands with these jasmines, these white jasmines.

I have loved the sunlight, the sky and the green earth;

I have heard the liquid murmur of the river through the
darkness of midnight;

Autumn sunsets have come to me at the bend of a road
in the lonely waste, like a bride raising her veil to accept her
lover.

Yet my memory is still sweet with the first white jasmines
that I held in my hand when I was a child.

Many a glad day has come in my life, and I have laughed
with merrymakers on festival nights.

On grey mornings of rain I have crooned many an idle
song.

I have worn round my neck the evening wreath of *bakulas*
woven by the hand of love.

Yet my heart is sweet with the memory of the first fresh
jasmines that filled my hands when I was a child.

35

榕樹

◆

THE BANYAN TREE

你這滿頭蓬髮，站在池邊的榕樹啊，你是否已經忘了那個小孩，就像忘了那群在你枝頭築巢又離你而去的小鳥？

你難道都不記得了？當年他是如何坐在窗前，驚異地望著你那扎入地裡的虯結樹根？

婦女帶著水瓶到池邊汲水，於是你巨大的黑影就在水面上扭動，彷彿一個掙扎著醒來的夢。

陽光在漣漪上跳舞，就像小小的梭，來來回回不斷織著金色的錦緞。

兩隻鴨子浮在自己的影子上，游過長滿水草的池邊。

面對此情此景，那個小孩當年曾靜靜坐著，陷入沉思。

他渴望化成一陣風，吹過你窸窣作響的枝葉；他渴望化成你的影子，隨著白日在水面逐漸拉長；他渴望化成一隻小鳥，站在你的最高枝上棲息；他渴望化成鴨子，漂浮在水草與光影之間。

O YOU shaggy-headed banyan tree standing on the bank of the pond, have you forgotten the little child, like the birds that have nested in your branches and left you?

Do you not remember how he sat at the window and wondered at the tangle of your roots that plunged underground?

The women would come to fill their jars in the pond, and your huge black shadow would wriggle on the water like sleep struggling to wake up.

Sunlight danced on the ripples like restless tiny shuttles weaving golden tapestry.

Two ducks swam by the weedy margin above their shadows, and the child would sit still and think.

He longed to be the wind and blow through your rustling branches, to be your shadow and lengthen with the day on the water, to be a bird and perch on your top-most twig, and to float like those ducks among the weeds and shadows.

36

祝福

◆

BENEDICTION

祝福這小小的心靈，這潔白的靈魂——他為大地贏得天堂的親吻。

他愛太陽的光，他愛看媽媽的臉龐。

他還沒學會蔑視塵土，也還沒學會渴求黃金。

緊緊擁抱他在你心上，祝福他。

他來到這片大地，數百條道路交相雜錯的大地。

我不知道他是如何在人群中選了你，到你門前，握著你的手問路。

他將會跟隨著你，一路上說著笑著，心裡沒有絲毫懷疑。

珍惜他對你的信任，引導他走上正途，祝福他。

把你的手放在他的頭上祈禱：即使下界的浪濤愈形凶

險，來自天上的風將會前來灌滿他的帆，助他航向平靜
的避風港。

　別在匆忙之中遺忘了他，讓他來到你的心中，祝福他。

B LESS this little heart, this white soul that has won the kiss of heaven for our earth.

He loves the light of the sun, he loves the sight of his mother's face.

He has not learned to despise the dust, and to hanker after gold.

Clasp him to your heart and bless him.

He has come into this land of an hundred cross-roads.

I know not how he chose you from the crowd, came to your door, and grasped your hand to ask his way.

He will follow you, laughing and talking, and not a doubt in his heart.

Keep his trust, lead him straight and bless him.

Lay your hand on his head, and pray that though the waves underneath grow threatening, yet the breath from above may come and fill his sails and waft him to the haven of peace.

Forget him not in your hurry, let him come to your heart and bless him.

37

禮物

◆

THE GIFT

孩子，我要送你一點東西，因為我們都在這世間之河裡漂流。

我們的生命會被帶往不同的方向，我們的愛會被遺忘。

但是我沒那麼傻，以為我能用禮物收買你的心。

你的生命正年輕，你的道路還很長；你一口飲盡我們端給你的愛，轉身從我們身邊離開。

你有你的遊戲，你有你的玩伴。假如你沒時間也沒心思留給我們，那又何妨？

我們老了，我們有足夠的閒暇細數逝去的日子，在心

裡珍惜那些從我們手裡永遠失去的事物。

　　河流她唱著歌迅速流走，一路突破阻礙重重。高山留在原地，他記得河流，用他的愛追隨河流。

I WANT to give you something, my child, for we are drifting in the stream of the world.

Our lives will be carried apart, and our love forgotten.

But I am not so foolish as to hope that I could buy your heart with my gifts.

Young is your life, your path long, and you drink the love we bring you at one draught and turn and run away from us.

You have your play and your playmates. What harm is there if you have no time or thought for us.

We, indeed, have leisure enough in old age to count the days that are past, to cherish in our hearts what our hands have lost for ever.

The river runs swift with a song, breaking through all barriers.But the mountain stays and remembers, and follows her with his love.

38

我的歌

◆

MY SONG

孩子，我這首歌會以樂音環繞你，就像一雙充滿愛的臂膀。

我這首歌會輕觸你的額，像一個祝福的吻。

當你獨自一人，這首歌會在你身旁坐下，在你耳邊呢喃低語；當你處在人群之中，這首歌會在遠處護衛著你。

我的歌會像通往夢想的雙翼，載著你的心前往未知的境域。

當黑夜籠罩你的路，我的歌會守護著你，像你頭上那顆忠實的星。

我的歌會安坐在你眼中的瞳仁，引領你的目光進入所有事物的核心。

當我的聲音在死亡之中沉寂，我的歌會活在你躍動的心裡，對你說話。

THIS song of mine will wind its music around you, my child, like the fond arms of love.

This song of mine will touch your forehead like a kiss of blessing.

When you are alone it will sit by your side and whisper in your ear, when you are in the crowd it will fence you about with aloofness.

My song will be like a pair of wings to your dreams, it will transport your heart to the verge of the unknown.

It will be like the faithful star overhead when dark night is over your road.

My song will sit in the pupils of your eyes, and will carry your sight into the heart of things.

And when my voice is silent in death, my song will speak in your living heart.

39

兒童天使

◆

THE CHILD-ANGEL

他們吵鬧鬥爭，他們懷疑絕望，他們不知道爭論何時結束。

我的孩子，讓你的生命降臨到他們之中，像一道沉穩純淨的光，讓他們因此感到喜悅，讓他們因此平靜下來。

貪婪和羨妒讓他們變得殘忍，他們的話語猶如嗜血的藏刀。

我的孩子，去站在他們憤怒的心中，讓你溫柔的目光落在他們身上，像黃昏那充滿寬恕的寧靜平撫了白日的紛擾。

我的孩子，讓他們看到你的臉，讓他們因此了解所有

事物的意義；讓他們愛你，讓他們因為愛你而彼此相愛。

　　我的孩子，來坐在無限的胸懷裡；在日出時刻開啟你的心扉，提振你的心靈，有如逐漸綻放的花朵；在日落時分靜靜垂首，完成一天的敬拜。

THEY clamour and fight, they doubt and despair, they know no end to their wranglings.

Let your life come amongst them like a flame of light, my child, unflickering and pure, and delight them into silence.

They are cruel in their greed and their envy, their words are like hidden knives thirsting for blood.

Go and stand amidst their scowling hearts, my child, and let your gentle eyes fall upon them like the forgiving peace of the evening over the strife of the day.

Let them see your face, my child, and thus know the meaning of all things; let them love you and thus love each other.

Come and take your seat in the bosom of the limitless, my child. At sunrise open and raise your heart like a blossoming flower, and at sunset bend your head and in silence complete the worship of the day.

40

最後的交易

◆

THE LAST BARGAIN

早晨，我走在石頭鋪成的街上喊著：「來雇用我吧！」

國王手持寶劍，乘著雙輪馬車而來。
他握著我的手說：「我用權力雇用你。」
但是他的權力我看不上眼，於是他乘著雙輪馬車離開。

正午，房屋靜立在炎熱之中，戶戶門窗緊閉。
我在彎彎曲曲的巷弄之間隨意漫步。
有個老人提著一袋黃金走來。
他沉思了一會，對我說：「我用錢財雇用你。」
他一個個地秤著他的錢幣，但是我轉身走開。

黃昏，花園的樹籬開滿了花。
美麗的少女走出來，對我說：「我用微笑雇用你。」

但是她的微笑褪了色，化成了淚水，於是她獨自回返
黑暗。

陽光閃爍在沙子上，海浪肆意灑落。

有個小孩坐在沙灘上玩貝殼。

他抬起頭，彷彿認得我似地對我說：「我用空無雇用
你。」[23]

我跟那位小孩在遊戲之中訂下的交易，讓我從此獲得
自由。

---

23. 這首詩頗引人深思。詩分五節，首節是個引子，接下來分成四節，前三
　　節描寫國王、老者、美女分別欲以權勢、金錢和美色（「微笑」）雇用
　　敘述者，但敘述者對這三者都看不上眼。最後敘述者來到海邊，看到一
　　個彷彿認得他的小孩，而這小孩願意以「空無」（nothing）「雇用」他。
　　敘述者接受了這份「交易」，並且「從此獲得自由」。「空無」之所以
　　勝出，獲得敘述者青睞，並讓敘述者獲得自由，其原因可能是前三者（權
　　勢、金錢、美色）都是變化之物，不足為恃。詩人並未明說，但這一批
　　判仍可從第三節隱約推知，因為這一節提到少女的微笑馬上「褪了色，
　　化成了淚水」。

"COME and hire me," I cried, while in the morning I was walking on the stone-paved road.

Sword in hand, the King came in his chariot.
He held my hand and said, "I will hire you with my power."
But his power counted for nought, and he went away in his chariot.

In the heat of the midday the houses stood with shut doors.
I wandered along the crooked lane.
An old man came out with his bag of gold.
He pondered and said, "I will hire you with my money."
He weighed his coins one by one, but I turned away.

It was evening. The garden hedge was all aflower.
The fair maid came out and said, "I will hire you with a smile."
Her smile paled and melted into tears, and she went back alone into the dark.

The sun glistened on the sand, and the sea waves broke waywardly.
A child sat playing with shells.
He raised his head and seemed to know me, and said, "I hire you with nothing."
From thenceforward that bargain struck in child's play made me a free man.

譯者感謝詞

文／余淑慧

這是繼《漂鳥集》之後，我與舍妹淑娟再度合作的翻譯詩稿。《漂鳥集》的工作方式是由我初譯，淑娟最後爲我潤稿。這次的工作方式與上一次相反，而且還加入了一位年輕的合作者：這次的四十首詩裡，前二十首由淑娟初譯，後二十首分別由我與小女茂嘉初譯，最後再由我統整校譯修潤。從一月到十一月，這份稿總共歷經十次修訂，而這份譯稿之完成，除了要謝謝淑娟與茂嘉的初譯，我還要感謝茂嘉和我的助理羿彤屢次幫我找出別字，錯別字與冗字等等。最後要謝謝編輯貝雯的耐心等待與敦促，還有漫遊者出版社願意給我們時間與機會，讓我們在泰戈爾的詩歌世界裡再度悠遊一年。

插畫家的話

文／吳怡欣

　　這本詩集的多首作品是透過孩子的視角出發來想像，詩人筆下也經常出現花草樹木或是大自然的意象，因此我在發想插圖時，除了加入些許童趣，也把大自然的事物融入構圖裡，在這六張畫作之中加以貫穿。

新月集
The Crescent Moon

作　　　者	泰戈爾(Rabindranath Tagore)
譯　　　者	余淑慧、余淑娟、陳茂嘉
內 頁 插 圖	吳怡欣
美 術 設 計	呂德芬
內 頁 排 版	高巧怡
行 銷 企 劃	蕭浩仰、江紫涓
行 銷 統 籌	駱漢琦
業 務 發 行	邱紹溢
營 運 顧 問	郭其彬
責 任 編 輯	張貝雯、林芳吟
總 　 編 　 輯	李亞南
出　　　版	漫遊者文化事業股份有限公司
地　　　址	台北市103大同區重慶北路二段88號2樓之6
電　　　話	(02) 2715-2022
傳　　　真	(02) 2715-2021
服 務 信 箱	service@azothbooks.com
網 路 書 店	www.azothbooks.com
臉　　　書	www.facebook.com/azothbooks.read

發　　　行	大雁出版基地
地　　　址	新北市231新店區北新路三段207-3號5樓
電　　　話	(02) 8913-1005
訂 單 傳 真	(02) 8913-1056
初 版 一 刷	2024年8月
定　　　價	台幣299元

ISBN　978-986-489-983-8

Complex Chinese Translation copyright
©2018 by Azoth Books Co., Ltd.
ALL RIGHTS RESERVED

國家圖書館出版品預行編目 (CIP) 資料

新月集/ 泰戈爾(Rabindranath Tagore)
著; 余淑慧, 余淑娟, 陳茂嘉譯. -- 二版. --
臺北市 : 漫遊者文化事業股份有限公司
出版; 新北市 : 大雁文化事業股份有限
公司發行, 2024.08
　面; 　公分
中英雙語賞析譯註版
譯自 : The crescent moon.
ISBN 978-986-489-983-8(精裝)
867.51　　　　　　　　　113010390

漫遊，一種新的路上觀察學
www.azothbooks.com

大人的素養課，通往自由學習之路
www.ontheroad.today